S0-BIJ-456

Managing Back©

Mugged by Reality

By
Dan Angel
and
Mike DeVault

Forward by **Lee Iacocca**

Tassletop Publishing
1610 S. 31st Street, Suite 102-281
Temple, TX 76504

For Toodle, Moose and
the Snaggle Tooth Tiger
---DA

For J,S,R, and my
professional anchors R&R.
--MD

Table of Contents

FOREWORD

The pace of change in the business world has never been as fast as it is today. Global competition is forcing fundamental changes in virtually every industry. And any business that is slow to adapt is courting disaster.

That's why *Managing Back: Mugged by Reality* is a great read for current and future business people. It's a proactive primer on management in the 1990s.

Managing Back: Mugged by Reality offers a concise collection of examples of where business organizations have gone wrong, and where they're going right. It also offers a useful "toolbox" of strategies and ideas that management can use to aggressively take charge of its business in order to start creating their own success.

Lee Iacocca

Introduction

He didn't know where he was going when he left. He didn't know where he was when he arrived. He didn't know where he had been when he got back. And he did it all on someone else's money. He was the man whose voyage transformed East and West. The "he" was Christopher Columbus.

American management has too many Christopher Columbuses. Instead of the Nina, Pinta or Santa Maria they are attempting to navigate modern day management seas in an old and outdated mass production vessel.

The future of American organizations will depend on management based on breakthrough thinking. Columbus was searching for a new world. Today's new world is in management. Unfortunately, too many organizations in business, education, and government are time warped. Even more unfortunate is the fact that they don't have a **clue**.

It isn't Mr. Plum with the lead pipe in the library. It is Frederick Taylor with mass production in the 90s. That is the crime of our time.

The 1980s clearly were the end of an era.

Management's new world is a place where management practices of the past will be self destructive. In the new world, competition, quality, innovation, customer service, and organizational survival will depend on how management is **practiced**. From the small business to the college campus to the multinational corporation, those who succeed will do so with an entirely new *bag of tools*. Links to the old world must serve only as a basis for **transformation**.

The management books that line the shelves in our nation's bookstores represent substantial variations in quality. Many present conflicting advice, or warmovers. Some provide only outdated material. If you had the time to read all the books, articles, and newsprint that weave today's management story together you would likely discover the **essence** of what is going on out there. **We've done that for you**.

After doing the research, analysis, and synthesis for *Managing Back: Mugged by Reality*, we know with much greater certainty that the traditional approaches to management are obsolete. The indicators are too powerful to ignore. *Managing Back: Mugged by Reality* is a radical attack on classic management.

Years ago Edgar Dale used a geometric figure to illustrate his concept of the "cone of experience." His point was that you can *tell* someone how to do something. A more effective way is to *show* them how to do it. Dale concluded that the very best way is to have the person **do it themselves**. It is our hope that you can take the material from this book and achieve Dale's highest expectations.

It is time to leave shallow management, chart a **new** course, and travel with a greater depth of understanding. The voyage to date has taken us from **craft** to **mass** production. Now we must move from **mass** to **lean**. Along the way we have created a hodgepodge of conflicting practices that are dependent on **more** rather than **less**.

Because today's requirements are consistently tougher we must change several practices **simultaneously**. These practices are examined in *Managing Back: Mugged by Reality*.

Managing Back: Mugged by Reality is divided into three sections.

Part One shows us how we were *Mugged by Reality.*

Chapter one, *A Bucket of Ice Water,* exposes us to the global village where we face the rude awakening of competition.

In Chapter two, we greet the ghost of management past and present. Clearly Old Taylor is past his prime.

Chapter three takes us back to *The Last Picture Show* for a dose of down-home wisdom. *When You're Ripe .... You Rot* examines the natural process of rotting which occurs in life cycles.

Mega Myths exposes nine fallacies in management thinking. *Placebos* puts to bed our over utilized excuses. *Going Bare* describes the economic cliff we are rapidly approaching.

Screwing Down is Screwing Up takes us **inside** the structure of American organizations. Chapter eight introduces a new challenge: *Ridology,* a subject worth studying.

In Chapter nine, we meet a popular children's character: *Waldo.* If you don't know him you should. If you remember playing Hide and Seek as a child, the meeting will be pleasurable.

Part Two is directed at discovering Zeitgeist (the management **essence** of our time). The new mind set begins in Chapter 10.

Chapter 11 introduces the *I-T-A Chain.* It all starts with a visit to grandma's house. Then a *Popcorn* snack (Chapter 12). In Chapter 13 we aim to *surprise and delight* you.

Time's a wasting. If you're not fast enough, *Poof!* You're gone. Learn the lesson of speed in Chapter 14. Downsizing isn't enough. Learn the difference of *downpowering* in Chapter 15. Your Zeitgeist won't be the same without it.

Charles Dickens wrote a novel called Great Expectations. Chapter 16 reveals a new meaning for his classic work. *PSSST!* These letters are more than just a funny sound. **Listen** to Chapter 17.

In Chapter 18 we enter the corporate battleground. Someone once said that War is Hell. Meet the combatants in *Warriors*. Shakespeare posed the question, "To be or not to be?" He didn't offer the answer. We do in Chapter 19, *The Land of Lean*.

Part Three is *Managing Back*.

Chapter 9 introduced *Waldo*. In Chapter 20 *Waldo* is found in eight Zeitgeist management contexts. The admonition is that Waldo doesn't stay in the same place very long.

Tools offers 28 important new breakthrough methods for you to use in this decade. No manager can afford to be without our *Bag of Tools*. In the final chapter, *The Zeitgeist Manager*, the curtain opens. It is time for **you** to direct **your** organization's destiny.

Writing this book has brought us great pleasure. It's been hard work, but we **know** it's a valuable addition to the management work currently available. It's nice to finish a book that you feel so **good** about. We hope everyone who reads *Managing Back: Mugged by Reality* will have common perspective, deeper understanding and the confidence to "do it."

The voyage of Columbus was difficult and treacherous. It was filled with risks. The voyage of modern management will be no different.

Columbus got all the credit but there were many others who worked as part of the crew and helped make the voyage possible. There wouldn't have been a new world without them.

We had an important crew, too. Our thanks to the best shipmates writers could have. Kay Barclay, Peggy Green, Virginia Boyd and Susie Zienko worked long hours at the computer. They also did some important editing. We wouldn't have gotten very far without them.

To David Everett our sincerest thanks for his wisdom and the wealth of stories he offered. His suggestions greatly improved the manuscript.

Our deep appreciation also to Larry Jenkins, Julie Todaro, Toma Iglehart, Linda Clement, and Holly Koelling.

There were those who were willing to talk to us about what was going on with their companies. Don Beaver at New Pig Corporation helped us find the pork. His insights and values were so refreshing that it was hard not to hog his time. Jerry Carlson of IBM answered all our questions with candor and helped keep us on the right track. Ditto for Gene Stouder at Motorola.

We also appreciate the time and information provided by Chris Bridenbaugh at Nordstrom, Richard D'Agostino at Personal Financial Assistant, Inc., and Gordon Lambourne in Marriott's Hotel, Resorts and Suites Division.

Each generation has its heroes. **Lee Iacocca** is certainly one of ours. His interest has made this book special. We thank him for his time, insight, and generosity. He is truly a 20th century corporate icon with a heart as big as his well-deserved reputation.

Finally, to the many organizational leaders who have recognized the need for a new order we offer our appreciation. We hope others will join with us in forging the response to zeitgeists that lie ahead!

Dan Angel and Mike DeVault
January 22, 1995

Part I

Mugged by Reality

1

A Bucket of Ice Water

*"The mid-80s was the twilight
of mass production."*

James P. Womack
The Machine that Changed the World

The United States of America held a fistful of aces and a few extra wildcards in the economic poker game at the end of WWII.

Our home market was **eight times** larger than any other market in the world. We were the wealthiest country in the world. Our technology was superior. We had a large skilled work force and our management know-how was most favorable when making world comparisons. In addition we had set up large manufacturing processes for WWII that could be easily converted for domestic non-war manufacturing needs.

Consequently, in the late 1940s the United States could boast more than 60% of the total world manufacturing goods and even 40% of total electricity. Our mass production system was working so well that our productivity grew 3.5% yearly average until the mid 60s.

Between 1965 and 1973 we grew at a 2% productivity clip. Only the oil embargo of 1973 seemed to make a difference and caused an actual minus in the productivity growth chart of 1974.

In the late 70s and throughout the decade of the 80s, our productivity growth slipped to **less than 2%** and became an issue of great concern throughout America. In 1991 it was **zero**. What made the smaller margin weigh even heavier on public awareness was the fact that we could increasingly hear the formerly faint productivity footsteps of other nations. First at a few decibels. Then double. Then treble.

What are the lessons of the 1980s?

First, white-hot **competition**.

For 35 years after WWII we didn't know about, care about, or worry about the competition. The 1973 oil embargo was an omen, a warning, a harbinger that a more balanced world economy was rapidly approaching. As a report from the Secretary of Labor concluded in June 1991, "OPEC in 1973 signaled the end to the U.S.A.'s dependence on itself. Since then the lessons of globalization and interdependence have been reenforced in many ways."

In an odd sort of way the U.S.A. could be typified by Newton's first law of motion. We were a body at constant speed and were likely to remain that way until acted upon by external forces: Japan, Germany, and now others.

In 1973 we crossed over into the economic twilight zone: competition.

To survive that competition, it would take much more than the traditional three Rs: reading, writing, and arithmetic. The new and extended R-list would be composed of reforming, regenerating, restructuring, retooling, revitalizing, reconceptualizing, reorganizing, redesigning, reconstructing, and reinventing.

We would now have to think in terms of three futures: possible, probable, and preferred. To reach the latter, would mandate turning ourselves into high productivity organizations. During the decade of the 70s, we were obtuse and arrogant. During the early 80s our Rip Van American management began to awaken. Only during the late 80s did we really begin to shed some of our lethargy. The competition **will** bring out the best in us.

The second lesson is that our **expectations** were too low.

David Kearns, chief executive officer of the Xerox Corporation, was one of the earlier discovers of America's LEL (low expectation level). After one of his numerous visits to Japan, he tried to isolate what specific things were different between Japanese and American managers. Finally, he penned the word **expectations**.

While Kearns was in Japan, General Motors let it be known that they were about to initiate a $10 billion quality and reliability improvement plan.

The reaction to this news at Toyota Motor Corporation was a bit unsettling. Accepting the news at face value, Toyota quickly reevaluated every current goal and ratcheted it **upward**.

Would American management be so adept at increasing their expectations?

For all the decade of the 70s and much of the 80s, American managers have been trapped in their own **nine-dot handcuff**.

Look at the nine dots below and try to connect them with one continuous, intersecting line that does not go in more than four directions. (Appendix A)

•   •   •

•   •   •

•   •   •

More than likely, Japanese managers would pass this exercise at a far greater ratio than American managers. Why? Because the answer involves **going outside** of the dots—a change in expectations.

The third lesson came the hardest. **We were doing it wrong**.

Somewhere our horn of plenty mass production system had run amuck. We had a major **design** flaw. How could it be that our **quality** wasn't good enough or that our **speed** was not world class?

For most of the 20th century our management had grown robust on mass production tools and techniques. By 1970 we were inebriates who didn't recognize we had a problem. We were on a 70-year bender and we couldn't stop drinking.

America was suffering then and **is still** suffering now from a massive Taylor-Ford hangover.

The decade of the 80s hit us like a bucket of ice water!

2

Old Taylor Past His Prime

"American-run businesses appear to be locked in some kind of cultural trance."

Joseph H. Boyett
Workplace 2000

Eighty years ago Frederick Winslow Taylor wrote *The Principles of Scientific Management.* His book and thinking influenced the development of mass production in the United States. Today he is remembered as the father of scientific management.

Old Taylor

Back in 1911 Taylor was exploring the problem of "underworking" (people who worked too slowly). He viewed this as coming from two causes: (1) people were naturally lazy, and/or (2) management didn't really know how to do a task so they had no idea how much time it should take.

Taylor was concerned with what he called **ordinary** management that consisted of doing things in a haphazard, unsystematic, or even casual way. Taylor saw the system of **craft** workers as very undesirable. Because craft workers did things differently, there was a lot of waste and inefficiency, he reasoned.

Why not, he thought, study the best way to do something and then do it that way?

Down with the old rule-of-thumb, one-by-one craftsmanship approach. Instead managers would take a new **scientific** approach: discover the best way and then show workers how to do it.

To Taylor the ultimate was doing something in an **absolutely uniform** manner. Managers faced the major task of gathering all of the traditional data (knowledge) and rendering how-to rules into scientific laws. That's why he called his process the new **scientific management**.

One amusing experience that had a lot to do with shaping his thinking came from studying a crew of men loading pig iron for Bethlehem Steel. The crew of 75 averaged 12 long tons of pig iron per man per day. After serious study Taylor concluded that each man **could** load about 48 long tons per day. This would be a quadrupling of productivity if it could be brought about. Taylor's technique may be a little outdated, but it worked in 1911.

He looked over the 75 men and studied 4 that were the best physical specimens. He examined each of these four men in terms of their character, habits, and ambition. One of the four men had enough energy to trot home (a distance of one mile) after working a full day.

Taylor focused on **Schmidt**.

In language that seems almost humorous by today's standards, he approached Schmidt and asked, "Are you a high-priced man?" He proceeded to offer Schmidt $1.85 a day instead of $1.15 (a 60%

increase). Schmidt said he **was** a high-priced man!

After Schmidt had more than tripled his rate of loading pig iron, one employee after another joined him at the new pace (and new wage). Soon the whole group.

But Taylor did much more than study the steel industry.

In 1878 he began as a day laborer at Midville Steel. He became a clerk quite by accident when the incumbent was fired for stealing. Later, because of his own high productivity rate, he became lathe boss. Eventually, he made foreman and decided that some changes should take place in the system of management. That is when he came up with the time-study method used for the pig iron study.

Basically, there were four elements of Taylor's scientific management:

1. Management had to study and develop rigid rules for cutting wasted motion and perfecting standardization in all elements in the working environment;
2. Workers had to be carefully selected and trained. Not only that, but you kept only those who performed;
3. These first-class workers needed the constant help of management who (with incentives) would help them work at a steadier and faster pace; and
4. The managers managed and the workers worked.

Enter Henry Ford

Henry Ford was only sixteen when he hiked the ten miles from Dearborn to Detroit looking for a job in one of the shops. A technological genius, he had it in his mind to build a gasoline powered vehicle. By 1883 he had built his engine. In 1896 he completed his "quadricycle." You guessed it—a horseless carriage.

But bigger times were in Ford's future.

In 1908 Ford proclaimed that he would build a motor car "for the great multitude," and introduced the Model-T. Over the next 20 years he sold **17 million** such vehicles.

Ford learned a great deal from the principles of scientific management and time-study methods introduced by Frederick Winslow Taylor. His genius was putting it all together and developing a living and breathing **mass production system.**

In 1913 Ford opened a new plant in Highland Park, Michigan. To the marvel of everyone he was able to deliver parts in precise timing with need to a constantly moving conveyor belt (assembly line). Ford could turn out one completed vehicle every 93 minutes, **eight times** as fast as the old standard.

These mass production methods allowed Ford to double worker's pay to $5 a day in 1914 and to **lower** the price of a Model-T (from $950 in 1908 to less than $300 in 1927).

These methods soon became the envy of the world.

Mass production is based upon a number of component parts, but the basics are Taylor made. Trying to conceptualize the very best way of manufacturing a widget, you try to take the best of the craft and put it into a production process. The goal is to cut out any wasted motion and save time. This yields a higher quantity at a lower cost.

Parts are standardized, worker skills are unnecessary, and labor is divided into simple, easily repeated steps. There is a continuous flow of work, and parts are delivered to the worker. Tools are designed precisely for the single task to be performed. Workers do the same task in the same way hundreds of times a day.

Although Fred Taylor and Henry Ford did not produce the machine that spun straw into gold, their system came close to it. Automobiles and other items became plentiful, people were paid higher wages ﹀because of the mass production system, and for the next 70 years not only was there nothing better, there wasn't even an Avis. The mass production system was largely adapted to offices, banks, schools, universities, hospitals, hamburger stands, government and everything else.

Ford and Taylor gave America its middle class. The duo stamped a Made in America ingenuity seal of pride on our national product.

But like the observer of uniform stone for a large unending fence, there is something that doesn't love a wall and wants it down. For the last decade, and maybe the last two, mass production as we know it has gone the way of the Berlin Wall.

Why?

3

When You're Ripe .... You Rot

"Nothing is more vulnerable than entrenched success."

George Romney

The Last Picture Show

Anyone who saw the movie *The Last Picture Show* can probably still visualize the brick mainstreet in the dusty west Texas town where the film was made. The turn-of-the-century buildings haven't changed much over the years and remain a visible reminder of better days.

Those who have traveled in Texas realize there are many places that resemble the town in the movie. Towns which have long since lost their vitality but not their spirit. Places where the football stadium is still filled on Friday nights and neighbors care about each other. Places, no more than dots on the map, that belong to another time, another place.

It was in a *Last Picture Show* town where the sign was first seen. Obviously intended to send an important message, its message was not clear to a youthful perspective.

Surrounded on mainstreet by interesting places like Haney's Drug Store, Higginbotham-Bartlett Lumber Company, and the Joy Theater sat the *Roscoe Times*. Inside this nondescript dwelling, the sign hung proudly for all who cared to glance at its words of down-home wisdom.

Made from plaster (high style!) the sign's simple but thoughtful words spoke:

> "When you're green you grow....
> ....When you're ripe you rot."

Whether the message was intended to be an extension of a forgotten biology lesson, some deep philosophical principle understood only by adults, or, more likely, to cover a hole on the office wall, it worked. Whatever its original intent, this law of nature seems especially powerful today.

An apple turns from green to red, puppies grow into dogs, and loveable children change into intractable adults. Each stage bears little resemblance with its predecessor. At each evolutionary stage, new patterns of behavior are observed.

Organizations are like plants, animals, and people. They enjoy periods of growth, they stop growing, and then they rot. Unlike other organisms, however, they are capable of sustaining decay for longer periods of time.

The Morning Paper

Whether one reads the paper in the morning or late at night, the news is the same. The business headlines of the 1990s describe American organizations in a state of decay:

- Woolworth Trims 2,000 Jobs
- Citicorp Reports $885 Million Loss
- Bellsouth Reduces Workforce by 10,000 with More to Come

- Ailing Giant Places Big Bet on New Cars
- Southwestern Bell Offering Executives Incentives to Leave
- Allied Cuts 5,000 Jobs in Large Restructuring
- US Air to Seek Pay Cuts to Help off-set Big Losses
- AT&T Will Cut 14,000 Jobs to Help Pay for Merger
- United Technologies to Cut 250 Workers from Staff

One morning's business section brought the discouraging news that the number of banks will shrink 25% by the year 2000 due to oversupply and profit squeeze. American Airlines will trim capital spending by $2.5 million. The DuPont Chemical Company cut almost 1,100 jobs, and Pacific Telesis became the third regional Bell phone company in one week to announce management cutbacks.

On the TV news or in the newspaper examples like these dominate the headlines. The problem extends into service, small business, education, and government as well.

Even winners of the prestigious Malcolm Baldridge National Quality Award have had problems.

A 1990 winner, the Wallace Company, suffered through a 35% revenue decline. The Wallace Company CEO observed that you get walloped just when you think you have it made.

Indicators that many American organizations are still in decay persist:
- Productivity is not growing as fast as it once did. (1994 did show the best improvement since 1984 at 2.2%.)
- Companies are still not perceived to be world leaders in quality, service, and speed.
- Managerial talent that is no longer clearly the best in the world.
- Response to changing, competitive standards is not nearly as fast as it should be.

- Lack of innovation in product, process, and structure.
- Inability to get from innovation to production to market as quickly as demands warrant.
- Bloated structures that are incompatible with new global market conditions.
- A managerial mindset caught in the time-warp of production's "golden age."
- Emphasis on jobs rather than skills.
- Adherence to bottom-line thinking at the expense of other important factors.

Rotting is a natural process that occurs in all life cycles. Nature responds to these cycles by decomposing and recycling in order to grow anew. This is nature's way of regenerating; renewing its vitality. Organizations must also regenerate and renew. Only after organizations recognize their own decay can the process of change begin.

Mirror, Mirror

It is a lot easier to recognize decay in tangible organisms than it is to recognize it in a structure or process. Even when old machines are exchanged for new ones, the production process remains the same. American industry is in the process of reducing the number of workers it employs. Cutting jobs without consideration to other important aspects of the enterprise is useless. It simply leaves behind the same old structures with less friendly inhabitants.

There are no results inside an institution. In order to recognize decay within, **the focus should be outward**. The customer will usually provide the organization with the answer to the time tested question that begins, "mirror on the wall...."

Without giving it much thought customers expect regeneration to occur. When it doesn't, their loyalties are directed elsewhere. They are ready to embrace new products, services, improved levels of variety, and customization in response to their "obvious" needs. These consumer demands are available in the marketplace and customers will find them.

Too often consumers are left with updated versions of the same products and services they have become cynical about. Predictably the consumer view of progress is that it's a continuing effort to make the things we eat, drink, and wear "as good as they used to be." Despite the **lowered expectation** expressed in this view, many organizations find this minimal standard difficult to meet.

There are exceptions. One such exception is Florida's Disney World. Built upon citrus and swamp land sits America's number one honeymoon location. It is a place where, surprisingly, adults outnumber children 4 to 1. It is an organization whose annual revenue exceeds $2 billion. At a time when many peers are just beginning to recognize their own decay, this large, complex organization continues to prosper. Why? Michael Eisner, Disney's CEO, explains their simple principle: "We are in the business of **exceeding** everyone's high expectations."

Ask consumers what they like most about DisneyWorld and you won't hear parades, fireworks, or a ride through Space Mountain. When customers were asked to rate the top items at the theme park they cited friendliness of employees and cleanliness as the top two.

There really is some magic in the Magic Kingdom. This is an organization that understands what business it is in and never overlooks the little things.

Natural Beverages

In an era of takeovers, buy outs, mergers, and conglomerates (another sure sign of rotting), it is difficult to keep a sense of what business you are in. Smaller businesses generally do this better than large corporations. A Forbes study identified the 15 best little companies in America. The 15 were successful because they were able to exploit **niche markets**. They identified unfulfilled market needs and matched them with their organization's principal mission.

Large or small, organizations need an understanding of precisely what business they are in. It is much easier to move the enterprise toward fulfillment of the mission if everyone from the executive suite to the custodians understands the reason the business exists.

This essential question of raison d'etre was posed to the people at Perrier. Try to answer it on their behalf. Your first inclination is to suggest that they are in the bottled-water business. Wrong! Another possibility is soft drinks. Wrong again! Perrier is in the business of natural beverages. The distinction is subtle but extremely important. They found their niche market.

Knowing what business you're in is one step in the process of regeneration. It is not the only step.

Humpty Dumpty

The best seller, *In Search of Excellence* based its results of 43 companies on 20 years of success. These companies demonstrated superiority over their competition as measured by six yardsticks. Only five years after the book's publication, **two-thirds** of the companies were no longer on the pinnacle.

In the children's nursery rhyme, Humpty fell from the wall and all the king's men couldn't put him together again. Many of the two-thirds that lost their place in the success-line won't be put back together again either.

Why?

Because organizations seem to dwell upon past accomplishments.

The MIT Commission on Industrial Productivity found that managers and workers were so attached to the old way of doing things that they couldn't understand the new economic environment. George Romney, former CEO of American Motors, suggested that "nothing is more vulnerable than entrenched success." Apparently phenomenal success is at the root of the rotting process.

To some extent it is the very magnitude of past successes that has prevented adaptation to a new world. Seizing success as if it were something that can be placed on a shelf to be admired will lead to a common foible of successful organizations: Taking a good thing too far!

Sears is a classic example. Sears was mugged by the reality of declining sales and reduced market share. Fighting back, it cut 50,000 employees and closed 113 retail stores and 2,000 catalog outlets in a first effort strategy.

The Sears "Big Book" catalog, a mainstay throughout its history, ended its run. The passing of the "Big Book" is unthinkable to some but it is symbolic of the "rotting" that has moved Sears behind discounters Wal-Mart and K-Mart in the retailing parade. These changes are just the beginning. Once the cuts and restructuring are complete, Sears will still have to work very hard to carve out a successful niche in the retail marketplace.

In this tale of two companies, one old and one new, Sears will continue to experience the worst of times — at least for awhile.

Our fixation on *what is* obscures the necessary vision of *what isn't* and *what could be.*

Like the plaster sign in the Roscoe newspaper office, there are other gems of down-home wisdom that would have served as excellent advice to the companies who let their competitive, superior positions deteriorate.

One such example is: "It's what you learn **after** you know it all that is important."

Some organizations have found the truth in that quotation either out of financial necessity, survival, or both. For other organizations it was already too late. Of the companies listed in the Fortune 500 rankings 10 years ago, many are absent today.

Peaks And Valleys

General Motors was one company that stalled out during much of the 1980s and is now showing signs of renewed vitality. One good thing did happen to GM at the 1992 Rose Bowl Parade. GM's float won first prize. As an added bonus, the float entered by one of their chief competitors, Honda, broke down and had to be towed from the parade route. These token victories can't disguise the massive centralization which was one of their major problems. Organizations, like GM, needed to reconstruct, regenerate and revitalize.

They continue the painful process of doing so. Their North American auto operations recently produced its first profit since 1989. The company must continue to cut costs and improve productivity. GM remains largely a dinosaur unable to move quickly.

General Motors operates in a highly competitive global marketplace and their problems are a long way from being solved. GM, the dominant auto maker for many years, realizes what it doesn't know about today's marketplace. What it is learning now and how it changes because of what it learns will be most important. GM was late in spotting its decay and had a long way to go to catch up. Despite unprecedented efforts, the road back has been treacherous, time consuming, and costly. The restructuring begun at the end of 1991 was an important first step.

Ricoh could have simply enjoyed business success and market share in the copier field. Instead the company chose to do more with available technology. The end result? A copier, fax, scanner, and printer combined into one. Results like this come from a single-minded commitment to be the best. The Imagio series that combined these four technologies into one also represented "customization." Customers enjoyed a 60% reduction in the space necessary to "house" these essential office machines.

Apple Computer Company is working on a computer that combines phone, printer, fax machine, and copier. This home communications center will handle voice and electronic mail as well as process documents. Using the operating system of the consumer popular Macintosh, Paladin demonstrates the capacity of organizations to avoid the "bleeding edge."

Mature organizations are unable to improve rapidly. This is due primarily to the **sunken costs** invested in the status quo. These organizations will make major breakthroughs only if they are willing to innovate. Until the 1980s the dominant response of American industry to the changing global climate was a self-imposed determination to survive by past practices.

GM and Ricoh provide contrasting examples of organizations attempting to change to a rapidly changing global environment. In GM's case, much of the challenge is to **unlearn yesterday**.

GM is trying to radically alter the way it does business—from the way it develops new cars to the way it interacts with employees and dealers. In effect, GM and companies like it must concentrate significant resources on stopping the process of decay while the Ricoh's are busy inventing tomorrow.

This is the state of competition that exists today. Peaks of competition are everywhere. In February of 1994, Taco Bell introduced "Border Lights." This market response for a lower-fat product line includes tacos, burritos, cheeses, sour cream, and guacamole. Not only are the other fast-food chains watching, so are the nutritional experts. Remember McLean?

Packard-Bell, the company with approximately 50% of all home PC sales, continues to introduce new product lines. Compaq has introduced home PC's with the Pentium Chip. Hewlett-Packard and AT&T are also after the home PC user.

Competition in markets has reached unprecedented levels. The market winners are capable of changing quickly and meeting new market demands. The losers aren't sure what to do. The balance between what a company is or was and what it must be to survive and proper is delicate.

The difficulty for American business is to favorably alter this imbalance as quickly as possible. This requires tough-time changes. Tough-time changes are always painful.

Changes in job design, organizational structure, and availability of skilled workers are just a few of the categories that need the immediate attention of American organizations. These changes will continue to require a spectrum of sacrifice.

Too many American organizations are **still** decaying. The competition will always view them as "ripe for the pickin." It's a new culture for everybody. The mass production technology of the past will continue to lead many companies to continued rotting. Organizations need to re-learn and adapt anew. Some are making the changes very quickly and adroitly, others have been slow to change.

Organizations must follow the regenerative process so successful in nature or simply rot away. If it sounds ominous, it is.

Rotting is management's dead-end!

R.I.P...(e)?

Mega Myths

> *"Don't count your boobies*
> *before they hatch."*
> James Thurber

Several years ago James Thurber wrote a short story fable entitled "The Unicorn in the Garden."

The story presents a husband who constantly reports seeing a unicorn in the garden. Perplexed, annoyed, and exasperated, his wife eventually asks a mental institution to come and take her husband away.

When two looney bin officials arrive at the house, they immediately see the husband. He looks, sounds, and seems very normal to them. "A unicorn?" the husband says softly. "Why, the unicorn is a **mythical** beast."

The staff, convinced that he is quite normal, eventually strait-jackets the wife!

The unicorn **is** a mythical beast, but we constantly juggle between myth and reality: Santa Claus, the Easter Bunny, the Ground Hog, and other paraphernalia scattered throughout the American culture.

A few days before my daughter Shelby was to be six years old, we were sitting in a coffee shop.

The bright blue eyed little girl was sparkling at the idea of being <u>that</u> old and her older brother Scott dead panned "It isn't automatic you know?"

"What do you mean?" she demanded.

"Only if you have been good and Mother Nature and Father Time say you can," he said in the most stern and final way.

As the surprising news turned to fear and uncertainty, tears started to form.

"That's enough," I said. Mother Nature and Father Time are myths—they are not real." I assured my daughter that indeed she **would be 6**!

Remember when you were growing up? Where were you when you were invited to go on your first "snipe" hunt? Were you a Boy Scout? A Girl Scout? At a youth camp? Probably more than half of the American population has been exposed to this fun-loving hoax. Sometimes it is carried to such extent that participants pantomime actually catching "snipe," but they **never** show them to the intended victim.

America loves myths, but there are some that we should **shake**.

As we move toward the new 21st century economy of the 1990s, America suffers from nine mega myths.

Mega Myth One: **Mass Production is the cat's meow.**

Since Frederick Winslow Taylor and Henry Ford combined their talents in the early 1900s, mass production has been the sole mind set of American managers. In many ways it has become America's gift to the world. But just as **craft** gave way to **mass**, it is now necessary for **mass** to give way to **lean**. Starting in the 1970s and becoming crystal clear in the 1980s, mass production is no longer the way of the new economic world. Mass production is no longer **purrrrfect**.

Mega Myth Two: **First-time quality is not possible.**

Inherent in our way of thinking about mass production was a whole system of inspectors, supervisors, indirect workers, middle managers, defective pieces, imperfect products, extra storage space, and the word "**rework**." It was our assumption that in order to keep the production line moving, first-time quality was not possible.

That assumption is no longer valid. Under the mass manufacturing system, factories spend up to 25% of their budget in expecting, locating, and fixing mistakes.

First-time, every-time quality is not only possible in the 1990s, it will be **mandatory** if our products and services are to meet world standards.

Poor quality costs. It costs in terms of inspection, rework, inventory space, scrap, and customer dissatisfaction. Even in the mid 90s, many U.S. companies and manufacturers are spending several times their profit margin in poor quality the first-time products. The same can be said for services, government, and education at all levels.

Mega Myth Three: **If we build it, they will buy it.**

For years we have made the assumption that our customers will buy whatever we build. No matter that quality, design, or follow-up service was poor. The old philosophy may still work for Kevin

Costner in *A Field of Dreams*, but customer loyalty on the basis of poor quality, lack of competition, and a feeling of nationalism is a thing of the past. Customers today demand choice, convenience, and high quality in product or service.

Mega Myth Four: **Making it faster costs more.**

Numerous recent experiences have disproven this myth. Large bureaucracies at General Motors, Sears, and any number of other facilities have put needed decisions on a back burner waiting for some abstract higher up to say "Okay, go ahead." Several firms such as Cincinnati Milacron have found that if they produce something faster, they can charge a higher price. **Just in time** inventory is another way of cutting costs using speed.

Mega Myth Five: **Bigger is better.**

Mass production thinking was based upon vertical integration and economy of scale. No matter what your field of endeavor, it was assumed that bigger was always better. Sears, General Motors, and IBM have recently been on decentralization campaigns. The name of the game in **this** decade is competitive smaller pieces and parts.

Mega Myth Six: **Design precedes production.**

In our old way of thinking, we began with a grand design with a product or process and simply did whatever it took to produce whatever was designed.

Only recently have we discovered that design can be responsible for up to 80% of the cost of a product. Modern-day thinking allows us to work as a team where design can be simplified for production, allowing for better quality, faster production or processing, and better customer satisfaction.

Mega Myth Seven: **Frontline workers aren't important.**

The genius of mass production was breaking jobs into very small units and simple procedures where "anyone" could do it. Very little skill or education was involved and workers were as interchangeable as the parts they were assembling.

In **this** decade workers must know more, do more, and be fully integrated into the process. Educational funds will have to be distributed in a much different manner. The **frontline** worker is going to be the key to success.

Mega Myth Eight: **If we haven't got it, it can't be any good.**

Complacency? Slovenliness? Vanity? Probably. But the real reason **is arrogance**.

From the mid 40s and until the mid 70s, the U.S.A. had a nursery rhyme existence. We really did have the goose that laid the golden egg. It never dawned on us until the 70s that perhaps **our** goose needed goosing. There was no need to cross the ocean or even a nearby border to look at other **benchmarks** or processes that could be adopted for **continuous improvement** in our endeavor.

Mega Myth Nine: **Rules of the game stay the same.**

Jerry Carlson, IBM's Entry Systems Division vice president and general manager of the company's Austin plant, explains the fixation.

"Growing up in the U.S. through the 50s and 60s, I looked at things as they were. That's how it is, I told myself. That's my model because that's my experience base." But Carlson knows that times have changed. "The old constraints of time, space, and material are no longer there. We have to think totally differently about the opportunities."

Many of us are still playing with those 1950 and 1960 rules. We think the Monopoly game hasn't changed. While many of us are still trying to purchase Boardwalk, Japan is winning the economic competition in a cake walk!

The name of the game today is no longer Monopoly. It is lean. There is no Chance or Community Chest that will come to our rescue.

Only a **Zeitgeist** player is going to do well in the economic game of the 21 century.

These mega myths are worth repeating in quick summary fashion:
1. Mass production is the cat's meow.
2. First-time quality is not possible.
3. If we build it, they will buy it.
4. Making it faster costs more.
5. Bigger is better.
6. Design precedes production.
7. Frontline workers aren't important.
8. If we haven't got it, it can't be any good.
9. Rules of the game stay the same.

If we don't shatter these mega myths in the 1990s **we** will be a **bunch of boobies**!

PLACEBOS

"Too often we give excuses."

America's Choice: High Skills or
Low Wages

It used to be a common practice.

Aunt Debbie was lonely and went to see her country doctor. He talked with her, showed some interest in how she felt, and gave her a prescription.

Grandpa Ernest, although he was 80, didn't feel as well as he used to so he too sought out his family doctor. The doctor listened patiently and gave him some little yellow pills.

Cousin Edna, a full blown hypochondriac, called her doctor daily. She always had the symptoms of some new disease. If you opened her medicine chest, you would find bottles, tubes, vials, and containers that would compare well with a carton of M&M candy on the loose.

All of these people at one time in their lives (and probably more) received a **placebo**. Placebos are inert, inactive, and ineffective at solving what ails you. Although sometimes described as harmless, that would be inaccurate in terms of the placebos the American public is feeding itself concerning our new found world economic competition.

Let's take the same three folks that we introduced, take them out of their concern with personal health, and transfer them to concern with national economic health.

Aunt Debbie lived through WWII. She says that she is "not surprised" that the nations we defeated have rebuilt and are simply catching up. "We have to expect that," she says. "We couldn't always have it as good as we did back in the late 1940s and 50s."

Debbie has given herself a placebo. Reality says otherwise. In actuality several nations are doing **better** in comparison to the United States than they did before the war.

Grandpa Ernest worked for General Motors for thirty years before he retired. He rolls his eyes, arches his brow: "It's simple, those countries all **pay** less than we do," he says with complete conviction thinking that his articulation is irrefutable.

Ernie's problem is that he has given himself a placebo. He needs to look around and see how things really are. Germany and Italy both pay their textile workers more. In 1990 **a dozen nations** paid higher wages than the U.S.A. More than half of our trade deficit comes from nations that pay their workers **higher** wages.

Our hypochondriac friend has also supplied herself with a variety of excuses.

The red pills promise that our technology will save us. She clutches the container and thinks nothing of the fact that we have been unable to **apply** our technology.

She refers to the brown vial in her left hand and says that our problem is "We try to train everybody." Her inference is that we should only train the best and leave the rest. She obviously doesn't know that there is a worker shortage looming in the 1990s and that if people don't have an opportunity to earn for themselves then the rest of the society will have to pay in one way or another.

Finally, she refers to her favorite blue dosage container and speaks with great enthusiasm: "We don't have to worry too much, because our productivity has really improved in the last ten years."

Has our productivity **really** improved?

Certainly there are reports of it in many of our large manufacturing companies, but these reports are placebos, too. Much of our productivity gain has come through two-family incomes. In the past 20 years we have gone from having 40% of our people in the work force to 50%. Other gains have come from closing down plants that were inefficient, and downsizing or restructuring that has left in its wake five million Americans who are unemployed—and possibly unemployable.

As we are about to leave Aunt Debbie, Grandpa Ernest, and Cousin Edna, nosey neighbor, Snoop, throws in his two cents worth. Putting his hands on his hips in a defiant manner, he says, "There is absolutely nothing wrong with American management. We are not sick; we don't need to be cured. Everything will be fine when the economy gets better."

Neighbor Snoop is going through a three-part cycle that has gripped many of America's managers. It starts with **disbelief,** moves into **denial**. Finally, it reaches the **acceptance of reality** stage.

There is a new physician in town. This healer doesn't bleed patients and doesn't dispense placebos. He deals with the harsh realities of the new economic world. He or she is **The Zeitgeist Manager**.

The Zeitgeist Manager scours the world for new management medicine that will cure our ailing economy. He seeks Waldo and will discover Zeitgeist. He is the bearer of the elixir that will rejuvenate and revitalize America's management in the 1990s.

Going Bare

"Our current course of action is nothing less than national economic and social suicide."

Joseph H. Boyette
Workplace 2000

When my son, Scott, was three years old, my wife, Patricia, took a risk. She left him home with his father.

We played some games and laughed together for a couple of hours, then I sat down for a few moments to read the newspaper.

It wasn't long until one of the neighbors tapped on my open screen door and suggested that I might want to gather up my son. It seems he was having a great time playing Cowboys and Indians in the backyard—totally in the buff.

My Kingdom for a Cloth
One of my favorite childhood stories deals with a king's new clothes. The story goes something like this.

Once upon a time there was a king who was so rich that he had everything. He was also very vain. A tailor in the kingdom approached him and offered the king something that he could not refuse.

"Oh King," the merchant said, "I have invented a new material that is so majestic, regal, and pious that although all of we **ordinary** people can see it, it is not visible to your royal eyes."

The king saw nothing at all, but concluded that he must have it at once. Soon the tailor produced the new garment and the vain king wore it.

As it turns out, the king was foolish indeed. There **was** no material. And when the king went out in public he was naked.

My son, Scott, and the foolish king are not the only ones going bare.

Thank God I was Insured

Nearly 39 million Americans had no health insurance in 1992. The number is up more than 5 million since 1989 and is greater now than when Medicaid and Medicare were brought aboard three decades ago. In all likelihood the number will rise to 42 million **without** health insurance by 1995.

Fortunately, thousands of American homeowners and businesses **were** covered by property damage insurance in 1991.

Why?

Because insurance companies forked over more than $4 billion in order to compensate for damages.

One fire in Oakland, California in the fall of 1991 cost over one-fourth of the total.

Although this massive payout is comforting for those with insurance, there are some notes of concern.

Insurance actuaries establish rates that will be charged by estimating the costs of damages over a long period: typically, 35 years. A string of disasters over a shorter period of time could be problematic.

There is some reason for concern because **two** of the past few years have been actuarially exceptional. 1989 was the worst year on record with payouts amounting to $8 billion. When teamed with 1991, it might make you wonder when Old Mother Hubbard's cupboard will be bare.

In July 1991 Mutual Benefit Life Insurance Company was seized by New Jersey regulators. Officials of America's 18th largest insurer asked regulators to seize control to stop a run on company assets.

Although three other insurance firms had suffered a similar fate earlier in 1991, Mutual Benefit had more than $13 billion in assets, and was an industry leader. The company had a 150 year history and an established reputation.

Much of the public wrath regarding the failures, and Mutual Benefit specifically, relates to major rating companies' performance: A.M. Best, Moody's, and Standard and Poor. One month before the seizure of Mutual Benefit, A.M. Best was showing its highest rating of A+; Moody's was showing an A3 "good." Standard and Poor signaled the firm was A "strong." Only a fairly new arrival on the block, Weiss Research, ranked M.B. as "weak." Weiss does not rely entirely on financial reports filed with state regulators. It does its own research including evaluation of the company's management.

Management, method, and means has become a big issue among insurance regulators and the American public. They are wondering **if they are going bare**.

Sometimes such risks are taken by all of us. As the old adage goes, "It is not wise to put all of our eggs in one basket." In our investments, therefore, we purchase **portfolios** to diversify and spread the risks.

In business the vast majority of firms whether manufacturing or service carry liability insurance. Without it they take massive risks. In insurance lingo they are "going bare."

Several years ago the Sure Grip International Corporation in Southgate, California made a decision. Harry Ball, president of the multi-million dollar roller-skate and skate board manufacturing business, flatly declared that he was not spending another dime on product liability. He took this action because of the steep increase in product liability insurance premiums. Harry Ball has been lucky. Even though Sure Grip could be devastated by one humongous liability claim, his firm is still in business.

Naked Management

What does all of this have to do with management needs of the future?

Plenty.

One of the most startling conclusions of the report on the Commission on the Skills of the American Workforce in June of 1991 is that American management is still clinging to the old mass production form of work organization. By not changing management planning and thinking, 95% of our manufacturing, service, educational, and governmental organizations are "going bare."

The way we run our organizations in the early 1990s is like playing Russian roulette with a 20 chamber gun. Nineteen have bullets. One chamber is empty. We get to shoot first.

Our preoccupation with, loyalty to, and stubborn adhesion for the mass production mentality makes us like the old farmer who won the state lottery. "What are you going to do with all the money?", he was asked. He paused, scratched his head and replied: "I'm just going to keep on farming...until it's all gone."

There are times when it is o.k. to go without protection.

Not too long ago, a university professor and psychotherapist visited a home for the mentally insane. When she emerged from the one-hour tour, her husband who had been nervously waiting at the gate articulated his reason for alarm. "Are you sure it is safe to go on a tour like that all by yourself?" the professor asked.

The psychotherapist responded in a very unconcerned matter of fact fashion, "Don't worry," she said, "lunatics **never** get together."

The fact of the matter is that we can no longer allow ourselves to go bare.

Our national economic portfolio is not risk free. If Standard and Poor were to do an economic rating, there would be a massive run on company assets. America is headed toward an economic cliff. Unless management in all sectors starts to rethink, replan, and take action then unlike Sure Grip our going bare may cost us immeasurably.

Monumental Error

The Lincoln Memorial was opened for public viewing in 1922. The popular landmark attracts more than 1.2 million visitors each year.

The monument, left alone for some 70 years, is now surrounded by fencing, workmen, and scaffolds. Over the next year or two, it will be restored.

American management has a similar challenge after 70 years of mass production mentality. If we can't get our act together in the next three to five years, we will be making a monumental mistake!

7

Screwing Down Is Screwing Up

*"Shoot first and inquire after-
wards, and if you make mistakes
I will protect you."*

Hermann Goering

Back to the Future

People interested in what the world will be like or what skills will
be needed in the year 2000 have plenty to read. Opinions about the
21st century abound. Bookstore shelves are filled with examples of
new age prophets (or is that profits?)

The future is fashionable!

It wasn't long ago that another generation was preparing itself for
the prospects of a new century. It was a century that began with the
"naughty aughties" and Gibson Girls, produced two world wars, and
propelled the United States to a position of world prominence.

Agriculture, the common "industry" of the 19th century, was
replaced by man and machine. Individual craftsmanship was

moved aside for mass production. The 19th century forever changed the character of work and the nature of the workplace.

The 20th century continued the exhilaration born of the industrial revolution. A revolution that, over 70 years, had already produced phenomenal results. The Industrial Revolution worked. It was right for its time. It literally changed the world.

The time immediately after the turn of the century was one of optimism. Although the optimism was more surface than real, one writer seemed to capture it best.

Horatio Alger's 135 tales of hope and promise sold over 20 million copies and helped define the 20th century hero and the American dream. He wrote about individualism and prosperity and his works offered promising suggestions about human beings in a free society and what the harvest of **sweatequity** might produce.

Alger's works echo in the accomplishments of 20th century hero, Edward Harriman, who went from office worker to railroad tycoon, and Andrew Carnegie who exchanged the job of cotton mill "bobbin boy" for steel magnate.

In Alger's world, hard work plus a little luck equaled the heroes he wrote about. Unfortunately, forgotten in the equation were the qualities of adventure, daring, and persistence that helped make heroes of Henry Ford and John D. Rockefeller. Alger's works were fiction turned into myth. In the real American workplace there were only knights and peasants.

The inspired and perspiring!

(Un)Orthodoxy

This view of the *inspired* and *perspiring* aptly describes the essential separation of work from worker, function from process, and mental from manual skills found in 20th century organizations from past to present. This view spawned the management orthodoxy of this century. A management orthodoxy based on **division**.

Organizations were divided into those who do the work and those who supervise those who do the work. This separation grew out of the assembly line model begun by Henry Ford and became an integral part of the mass production mentality. Structures designed to perpetuate this separation quickly followed.

Our organizations were created **vertically**!

It is in the context of work and the supervision of work that the foundation of modern personality hierarchies began. Hierarchies were designed to systematically pair man and machine into a sequential order based on function. Order which was perceived to be necessary to control inputs and outputs.

The Hierarchical arrangement was based on the idea of intelligence (inspired) at the top and effort (perspiring) everywhere else. Thomas Edison suggested that work is 2% inspiration and 98% perspiration. If Edison had designed the traditional organizational pyramid, he would have turned corporate America upside down.

Hierarchy subsequently brought about the creation of an army of **guardians**, each concerned with his unit's functional results.

The United States industrial society was arranged to maximize productivity, reduce costs, coordinate work and worker, and as a result guarantee the continuation of the enterprise.

Many of the 50 largest American corporations in 1917 still appear in today's financial pages. Organizational continuity, the underlying goal of Frederick Taylor's scientific management principles and the goal of modern organizations today, has not changed much in the last 80 years.

The management orthodoxy that propelled the U.S. into global prominence during the industrial revolution leaves it chasing the competition on many fronts today.

On The Marx

Imagine Karl Marx (despite his being a classic recluse) joining in conversation with his comrades over circumstances that didn't work out as they intended. During the discussion someone asks, "What went wrong?"

Marx replies, "It's no accident, comrade."

This famous Marxist line best describes a century of conscious, deliberate actions purposefully taken by well intentioned individuals that continue to leave American enterprise competitively vulnerable as the 21st century nears.

Modern organizations are saddled with the dead weight of past practices that emerged when work and workers were separated by laws, rules, and orders authored in the name of organizational necessity.

Machines became more important than the persons running them. Success was based on what company could produce the **most**, not the one who could produce the **best**.

Organizations converged in structures, practices, and processes with little expectation of convergence in thoughts, ideas, and solutions.

Historically, American organizations were built along dimensions of the product chain rather than in an organization of **teams**.

Organizations still operate with **outdated beliefs**. Today's organizational arrangements continue to foster:

- A **gap** between line management and the executive suite
- A **belief** that structure and managerial style do not make a real difference
- An **underestimation** of human resources
- Skills in workers that are **vulnerable** to rapid obsolescence
- A preference for managerial **detachment**
- **Short-term** cost reductions rather than long-term technical competitiveness
- **Unimaginative** management with a bottom-line view

Peasant Thoughts

Organizations remain inhibited by ingrained beliefs, attitudes, and practices that stifle creativity, individual initiative, and workplace self reliance.

Yesterday's organizational heroes were defined primarily in individual terms. Tomorrow's heroes will have to be defined by teams, coalitions, groups, and networks that share information while **interacting** together, not apart.

Implicit in management theory from Taylor to Drucker, organizations placed a higher premium on knights than peasants. The competitive success enjoyed by the U.S. in the old economy came from the ability to simply improve production.

The new global economy derives success from quality, convenience, timeliness, customization and variety. This requires **collaboration** of knights and peasants, not artificial unnecessary separations.

The standards of competition in all sectors continue to change. Institutions must also change and change again. To control a mass production society and enhance its validity, it was incorrectly assumed that artificial organizational barriers were necessary. These barriers, constructed vertically along the hierarchy and horizontally along the assembly line, were necessary to achieve organizational goals. These barriers deprived organizations of their most valuable asset: **human potential**. Labor was seen as a cost, and managing labor through the creation of elaborate structures a necessity.

The "S" Word

Each generation of management felt compelled to add yet **another layer** to the structure that separated workers. More rules and regulations were imposed on the workplace. Functions were separated into discrete, often unrelated parts. Work was organized for production efficiency only. Machines became more important than the people running them. As a result, organizations developed a self-respecting working class without regard to income and economic condition and in the process inadvertently discovered the definition of the word screw:

Screw (verb): Twisting motion, to operate, tighten down.

Tightening has been achieved by applying the **traditional** management notions of **plan**, **organize, command, control**, and **coordinate**. These managerial behaviors, applied with Taylor-like scientific precision, have left modern organizations in a less competitive position. In other words, *screwing down* has "screwed up" American enterprise! Our organizations have become like the man who kept striking the same match because it worked the first time.

Reform in American business means that top officers must cultivate new skills and managerial style. Our managers must begin to break rank with 70 plus years of tradition.

The American worker can no longer be regarded as the disposable lighter of this generation.

It is time to loosen up! Not just as a response to employees but to the organization itself. Organizations need new levels of **flexibility** that traditional structures make impossible.

The industrial revolution worked. The assembly-line production system worked, too. That's right, they both worked (in the past tense). Something has changed. In fact many things have changed. Terms like Six Sigma, Just In Time inventories, and Computer Integrated Manufacturing have proclaimed the new order.

The new world is also comprised of cyberspace, internet, lasers, biotechnology, and communication technology. A beam of light is used to cut faster and finer. What used to be grown is now synthetically made. Today's satellites are yesterday's cable. In a changing environment, yesterday doesn't always fit well with tomorrow, but a necessary relationship continues to exist between past and present.

The three distinct periods of major development in America are the **agricultural** era, the **industrial** revolution, and the **information** age. The relationship between each period is similar to the frames in a motion picture. Separately they have only a narrow meaning, but **linked** they tell an important story.

The industrial revolution was dependent on agriculture. The information age depends on the industrial sector to manufacture its technology. Agriculture has become agri-business. What the industrial revolution becomes and how it supports the information age will define the nation's future success on many strategic fronts.

Those who suggest that there is a post-agricultural or post-industrial society have it wrong. To the contrary, there is an inescapable, necessary link between each important period. One builds on the other. Each one has to be **transformed** to fit the needs of subsequent periods.

New structures, new processes, and new thinking must continue to replace the old. It's time to trade infrastructure for quality of work life. That is one requirement that will help ensure the success of the information age.

Mass production through mass separation equals mass disaster for American corporate interests. It is time to bring the **team** together.

Living W(H)ell

For Americans to live well, our organizations must produce well. Whether it is a corporate giant, corner grocery store, or the neighborhood elementary school the phase applies. This country has prospered because it has produced well. The industrial revolution has served us well. Unfortunately, it is being replaced. Eras, like products, reach obsolescence.

Ask yourself how well you are living. Consider how well you will live in the future. More importantly, how well will your **children** and **grandchildren** live?

Your answer will speak volumes!

Like individual craftsmanship before it, the industrial revolution is making way for an age of information based on technology. As those a century ago, another generation is again preparing itself for the prospects of a new century. Unfortunately, remnants of the industrial revolution remain the fabric of the corporate, entrepreneurial, and service culture. Pop culture without the pop!

It has been said that the future is often defined by the best of what has been forgotten from the past.

Let's hope not!

American organizations must take purposeful and concerted **action** if they are to capture anew their competitive position of the past.

It won't be as **easy** this time!

8

Ridology

"Stop da music."

Jimmy Durante

An Invisible Barrier

American organizations have often pointed the finger in the wrong direction when seeking answers to their problems. Governmental regulation, squabbles with unions, unproductive workers, lower cost labor elsewhere, trade barriers and educational ineffectiveness are just some of the reasons they cite.

How these problems have been viewed traditionally and why long held mind-sets continue to haunt organizations can be illustrated by the story of the five silly fishermen.

One day five gentlemen go to their favorite fishing spot. The day brings them great success and each one catches enough fish for a feast. As they are readying to leave, the leader of the group counts the fishermen—one, two, three, four. He quickly declares that one of them is missing and must have drowned. Continued counting produces the same result.

About that time a little girl wanders into their midst and seeing their panic asks if she can help them. Hearing their story she knows at once what the problem is and offers to find their "missing" friend in exchange for the fish. They agree. She has them count off one, two, three, four, five as they jump into the water. Looking around they "re-discover" their lost friend. They willingly give the little girl their fish and leave happily.

The problem of the five fishermen is very similar to the situation in organizations. Management can't seem to scale the invisible barrier of the old mind-set. Once the fishermen decided that one of them had drowned, they weren't capable of recognizing their own error. The problem for American enterprise, be it corporate, small business, government, or education is a collective **inability to abandon** what no longer works. Something keeps pulling them back to the old mind-set.

Past Tense

Old mind-set!. . .Old mind-set!. . .Old mind-set!. . .The phrase is referred to so often in books and articles that one quickly assumes it has a universal definition. To the contrary, it is defined in **different ways** by **different people**.

To some it's an adherence to the status quo. To others its meaning implies a strict devotion to bottom-line thinking. And to yet others the old mind-set is the traditional hierarchical view of the organizational pyramid and all it represents about process, product, and people. Another equally valid interpretation is the blind continuation of skills and ideas. The "old mind-set" has multiple meanings.

However it is defined, it is a way of thinking which keeps organizations from reaching new levels of operational excellence. Excellence which is needed internally and externally.

The old mind-set represents **past tense thinking**!

Bandits

There are organizations which have exhibited the capacity to abandon tradition and rid themselves of ineffective past practices in order to find new success. One such organization is Motorola's Boynton Beach, Florida plant.

In the worldwide marketplace of semiconductors and communications products, **competitive advantage** is everything. Some organizations are even willing to **restructure** in order to achieve it! For years, competitive advantage came from producing more for less. Now it comes from such radical concepts as redesigned production, employee retraining, removal of workplace barriers, internal work teams, and external alliances.

Motorola found itself being forced out the pocket pager market by the Japanese. Pocket pagers, radios, and other communications products made up 35% of all Motorola sales. It was essential that the pager market not be lost.

Their response?

Use the best available information about Japanese manufacturing and combine it with Yankee ingenuity to produce a uniquely American product which would become one of the best selling pagers available. **Even** in Japan!

This successful program, named *Operation Bandit* moved production at the Boynton Beach plant from the traditional to megaspeed robotics. The **Bandit** operation fulfilled its mission. It has since given way to a new generation of processes, responses and ideas.

It left behind an important imperative for corporations. **Bandit** applied the principle of **learning from** the competition instead of fighting them. It demonstrated the capacity of organizations to adapt to a new culture and at least, temporarily, leave the old mind-set on the shelf. It showed that success can be achieved in new ways.

Head of the Class

Ridding ourselves of sacred traditions and entrenched practices is not easy. American corporations are not the only organizations which need to find the epicenter of changed ideas.

The *Oregon Education Reform Act for the 21st Century* exemplifies an education effort to produce a new mind-set. Nothing is as ingrained in the nation's consciousness as those four years of youthful innocence (if you're over 40, that's what it was) that we call high school. The Reform Act took aim at this most sacred tradition.

This bold initiative essentially abolishes high school in its traditional form and replaces it with one intended to produce students capable of acting on the world stage.

In the new "high school" students can earn a certificate of mastery in the 10th grade. The remaining two years would divide students into two tracks: college preparatory courses or on-the-job training mixed with academic work. The act will also abolish early grade levels and increase the school year to 220 days by 2010.

Summarized by the act's chief sponsor, the goal is to produce the best educated students in America by the year 2000 and the best in the world by 2010.

High school is part of the collective American psyche. It serves to remind people of a safer, more secure time in life. Whether the act succeeds in achieving its laudable goals is for future generations to decide. What makes the reform important is that it demonstrates a **willingness** to move away from a pleasant routine that **isn't** working.

Fun, Fun, Fun

Look in the index of any book written about management, organization, business, or leadership and see if the word *fun* can be found.

Fun is a word which is rarely used to describe the work experience. The bumper sticker that declares:

*"I OWE, I OWE, SO OFF
TO WORK I GO..."*

aptly describes the sentiment of many American workers toward a place where people spend a third of their adult lives. Work in the United States has been designed to fulfill the Calvinist philosophy that work is service. It is the "calling" that is most important.

The authors of the book, *This Job Should be Fun*, surveyed 12,000 workers. Twenty-four percent of non-management personnel responding to the survey described their offices or factories as a "prison."

The view of work as imprisonment is **not likely** to result in the level of sustained effort needed by American organizations.

The notion that work **can't** be fun is outrageous. Workers know instinctively that fun and work should not be separated. Workers know that there is a likely cause and effect relationship between fun and work.

The corporate culture should recognize people for **who** they are, not just **what** they are capable of producing. Work may never again be life's central tenet. In recognizing people for who they are, the American workplace should rid itself of the misguided idea that work and fun are incompatible. Fun implies play and play is useful.

Don Beaver, founder of the New Pig Corporation, used *fun* to take a dull product and make it successful. The company's principal product is absorbent materials used to soak up oil and grease from factory floors.

The *fun* starts with the company name. PIG came about as the result of testing thousands of quarts of oil spilled in the company warehouse. The testing area was always a mess. A sort of PIG pen.

The absorbent material is produced as a sock-like device which might best be described as an industrial diaper. There is the standard PIG used for normal grease and grime and the HAZ-MAT PIG which aids in the clean up of hazardous material spills. The company's address is Pig Place, One Pork Avenue. Its toll free hotline is 800-HOT-HOGS.

Their product catalog is called the "pigalog" and notes are taken on "oink" pads. Place an order for $300 or more and you'll receive a pair of "porker" boxer shorts. Not only do these eccentric behaviors accentuate the purpose of the business to employees, they allow employees to have *fun*. Beaver states, "we work at having *fun* at our own expense."

The California Raisins are known to millions of people. The commercials which featured them extolling the virtue of raisins rescued the raisin industry. Before these ads began appearing, raisin sales were dropping at a rate of 1% per year. The Claymation figures did not spring to "life" during some "think-tank" experience on company time, but instead during a **casual** outing among friends.

When the time came to present the Claymation figures to raisin-growers, the creators didn't have a taped presentation available. Instead they put on white gloves and lip synched their way through, "I heard it through the grapevine." The rest is history.

Their successful credo: "We don't take ourselves too seriously."

At Gortex, the makers of outdoor wearing apparel with the special fabric, employees are invited to create their own business cards, including job titles. Sample the business cards and you will find several "presidents," "wizards," and "fortune tellers." There are even "executive wizards."

Toys

Some of the most significant (and most profitable) tools of enterprise started out as toys. They evolved not from an interest in work but rather an interest in play. Gunpowder was initially used for fireworks not guns. Ballbearings are descendants of marbles. The gyroscope was invented as a specialized top. 3M Post-It notes evolved from a need to keep a bookmark from falling out of the inventor's hymn book. The idea for key punch cards used in early computer operations came from the piano rolls used for *play*ing music. Teflon came about from a search for an **ad**hesive and resulted in an **ab**hesive to which nothing sticks. One of the most significant contributions to the field of mathematics is Neumann's *Game Theory*.

The best work is a kind of play.

There should be a place within organizations for *play*. Work and *play* can live together happily and productively. *Play* is natural, expected human behavior with enormous potential for revitalizing the ailing workplace. It is time to rid organizations of the necessity of creating so-called workplace prisons. It couldn't hurt and might be fun!

Good Riddance

What is the point of ridology? There are a number of important indicators that suggest American enterprise is in trouble. Granted, there are exceptions.

Neither workers nor their companies want to be second best. It is simply **not** the American way. The workplace mind-set is still beset with outdated ideas, corrupted processes, ineffective models, and obsolete patterns of required behavior.

Ridology is a new way of thinking about the proverbial drinking glass. It doesn't really matter if the glass is half empty or half full. The issue isn't about **quantity**. The argument just serves as an unnecessary distraction. It's what's **inside** the glass and what **can be done** with it that matters.

Ridology is about moving on. Ridology is about moving on to new ideas and new ways of thinking. This is what will ultimately matter most.

The Starfish

Loren Eisley, the noted British scientist and naturalist wrote a book of essays called the **Star Thrower**. One of the essays goes straight to the heart of the discussion of ridology and why it matters.

Day after day Eisley observed an old man standing on the beach picking up starfish that had washed ashore. The old man would pick them up and cast them back into the water.

Knowing that thousands of starfish washed ashore everyday around the world, Eisley couldn't understand the old man's reason for throwing them back.

He finally decided to seek the answer.

Approaching the old man who had just picked up a starfish, Eisley asked him why he picked up these starfish day after day and cast them back to the sea. "It doesn't matter," Eisley said, "thousands wash up everyday."

Displaying the starfish in the palm of his hand the old man answered: "It matters to **this** starfish!"

Where's Waldo?

"A stone, a leaf, an unfound door."

Thomas Wolfe

The Child In Us

Since 1987, millions of children have looked for Waldo. Four "Where's Waldo" books have sold over 13 million copies! Not bad in an industry where the benchmark for a children's book is lucky to reach 50,000 copies.

For those who have lost or misplaced their "child," an introduction is in order. Waldo is a fictional character whose red and white striped shirt, knit cap, and spectacles are instantly recognizable to legions of young followers. He is in books and puzzles. He is in trinkets and hidden in liquid graffiti.

The trick is to **find him**!

Think of Waldo as the master "hide and seek" player. He is a wanderer who is found in the most interesting places cavorting with wonderfully benign characters who come to life through the sketches of Martin Handford, Waldo's creator. Each hiding place is meticulously designed to make finding Waldo a challenge.

Waldo And The Fish

Kids are better at finding Waldo than the average adult. They seem to be able to cut through the unnecessary to find the obvious. Adults, on the other hand are a lot like fish. The last thing a fish discovers is water!

Waldo is the midpoint between Ninja Turtles, Cabbage Patch Dolls, Barney and the Mighty Morphin Power Rangers. All of these toys did the same thing. They captured the hearts and minds of children around the world. With our globe shrinking and a world economy developing, Waldo adapted. He became Wally in England, Walter in Germany, Charlie in France, and Ubaldo in Italy. Waldo is the child; we are the fish.

A Symphony Orchestra

To children, this descriptive character is engaging because he is simple and likeable but imaginative. For adults, Waldo can symbolize much more. He serves to remind us that the best idea may be the one most overlooked. He reflects the perplexity that adults feel when making the right choice from competing ideas. **In reality, we are all looking for Waldo**. From individual adults to corporate giants, we are constantly searching, but rarely finding, Waldo.

Waldo represents the challenge of finding the right answer, or the correct approach. He represents an idea not yet developed or a plan not made. He symbolizes the correct structure or the effective process. Finding Waldo means organizing manpower and machines like a symphony orchestra. He is the commitment "to be the best."

Waldo is **breakthrough** thinking!

Weeding

The *Saturday Evening Post* was looking for "Waldo" as it attempted to preserve its place in the publishing world. It didn't work!

Western Union should have been looking for "Waldo" when it declined to buy Alexander Graham Bell's patents. We've all heard of American Telephone and Telegraph (AT&T).

RCA licensed several Japanese companies to make color TVs. That meant the end of such production in the United States.

General Radio remained committed to the technologies it knew best from 30 years in the test equipment market. The result? The golden adage "stick to your knitting" almost became an epitaph.

Numerous people spent twenty years in the 60s and 70s trying to decide which was best. Theory X or Y. Actually it didn't matter. We couldn't afford theory X anyway.

Federal Express attempted to supplant airplanes with satellite transmissions called "zap mail." It got zapped!

More than **two dozen** managerial techniques have been implemented and advocated since 1950.

Confused?

We have to be able to synthesize diverse information, weeding out the irrelevant, and then conceptualize it into a coherent picture. We have to find Waldo.

Why Bother?

Finding "Waldo" is not be easy. Burdened by minutia at every turn and inundated with information, we're left with more chaff than wheat. Yet there are plenty of reasons to want higher quality wheat.

The world has changed. The way organizations change will determine whether they win, or lose; prosper, survive or fail.

The background for finding our friend, Waldo, is covered with ideas, trends, issues, concepts, and notions. Toss in some models, theories, and paradigms too.

- There is a changing business order. The s**tructure** of the work place is being re-designed.
- **Middle management** is heading in the direction of the dinosaur. Toward extinction! The computer is smashing it.
- Organizations are being developed around **new concepts** such as work teams, downsizing, flattening, quality circles, and realignment.
- The strategic resource has changed from individual to **information**.
- There is a revival of the entrepreneurial spirit. **Intrapreneurship** has become an internal twin.
- From a diverse society will evolve a **variegated** work force.
- Global **competition** is no longer an expectation. It is a reality.
- **Growth** in technology and service will not diminish.
- **Stillborn** ideas cannot be tolerated.
- Quality must return to the **standards** of the craftsman.
- Customer **choice** will not be limited. It will expand to even higher expectations of quality and service.
- **Data** will replace anecdote in defining strategic direction.
- Strategy and structure will **coexist** with many other variables.
- Organizational excellence, product leadership, and customer "cults" **are not strategically exclusive.**

The Elephant and the Mouse

Revolutionary change is occurring in America's corporations. After wobbling through the 1980s, the meaning of global competition is clear, and **transformation** is underway in many quarters.

The corporate world understands that finding Waldo is essential to their long-term survival.

Corporate America shouldn't be searching alone. There are plenty of reasons for **education** and **government** to join the hunt.

American industry in many sectors has become demonstrably non-competitive by world-class standards in the last 40 years. So has the American educational system.

What is needed is a world class workforce with world class education and training. It won't happen if our major (and minor) companies like Motorola continue to teach 50% of its factory workers how to read and write.

U.S. firms will spend 25 million teaching workers skills that they **should** have learned in school. During World War II, the Army taught illiterate recruits to read in 6 weeks. Today, that goal is not achieved for everyone after **13 years** of school.

What Happened?

A high school diploma is viewed as evidence of staying power, not as academic achievement, and we're not doing well enough in recovering our 300,000 school dropouts either.

U.S. schools have been **designed**, like U.S. industries, to keep people in line and to carry out orders—not to encourage independent thinking.

Government is hardly better off. Who would argue with the notion that an elephant is a mouse built to government specifications. The perception is that very little works well in government.

The perception is not misguided when it is formed by Medicaid payments hundreds of times in excess of non-Medicaid charges for the same services or a $250,000 unpaid bill for meals and receptions in the House of Representatives dining hall. Maybe, there really is such a thing as a free lunch!

Social, economic, and cultural progress has historically been measured in terms of more or better or improved. None of these will define progress in the years ahead.

A better version of what doesn't work is like putting polka dots on an Edsel!

The shift must be to new paradigm expectations and the adoption of world class standards. The United States must join other nations in adopting High Performance Work Organizations in **all** sectors.

On The Right Track

Not everyone is on the wrong track. Many companies have heard the messenger, understood the message, and begun to make changes.

- The **Ford Motor Company** has implemented continual quality improvement (CQI) as a way to compete with foreign auto makers. "Quality is job 1" is much more than a television commercial.
- Rewarding employees for labor costs reductions and increasing employee participation to previously unheard of levels is well underway at the **Donnelly Corporation**.
- Steve Jobs left **Apple Computer**. He also left an important tradition, "We hire people who tell us what to do."
- The **Dana Corporation's** innovative management style can be summarized in a philosophy called "forty thoughts." The emphasis is on people.
- One company implemented an "Older Americans Program." Its goals were helping employees with retirement planning and temporary employment within the company after retirement. **Travelers' Insurance Company** had the vision to see the long-term value of human resources.

- **Westinghouse Electric Corporation's** Nuclear Technology Division recognized its changing environment and shifted to a **service** mentality and away from its previous emphasis on design.

Modern organizations have long been known for **tinkering**. There was a time when tinkering was sufficient. But tinkering has given way to **transformation**.

Vacuum tube radios became transistors. Transistors became stereo pocket radios which became compact disks and CD players. This led to optical disk computer memories. The vacuum tube was completely transformed.

Today there are hundreds of books, articles, workshops, and themes presenting a version of Waldo.

You are constantly invited to sample his wares.

This book finds Waldo in today's **management** context.

Part II

Zeitgeist

10

Being of Changed Mind

"Conform and be dull."

J. Frank Dobie

Weather

Certain things change often. Put computer software, diapers, music, waist size, moods, seasons, and postage rates into the "change often" category. Add in tastes, styles, hemlines, and the status of the ozone layer.

On the other hand, there are things which have remained constant. Consider the lasting nature of the Dewey Decimal System, bad habits, George Burns, the Ten Commandments, leopard spots, and the Thursday night TV lineup. Don't forget politicians kissing babies, congressional incumbents, the horrors of adolescence, and New Year's Eve celebrations in Times Square.

There are times when change is necessary and practical. There are other instances when a product is developed with such enduring qualities that it lasts.

Take Monopoly

The game featuring Milborn "Rich Uncle" Pennybags was introduced to Americans 58 years ago. It remains a cash cow for the Parker Brothers company which developed it. Since its introduction 100 million copies have been sold worldwide.

Monopoly's successful formula appeals to the basic instincts. It is a successful recipe of greed and desperation mixed with an unconscious desire to live the dream of a real estate mogul. It was Donald Trump before Donald.

In the early 1990s, Parker Brothers brought 5 regional tournament winners from across the U.S. together to face-off in the ultimate Monopoly challenge with the winner proceeding to the world championship in Berlin. In the irony of the most recent competition, the winner was an investment banker.

Another example of sustained excellence and tradition can be found in the corporate symbol of RCA. Nipper, the dog who stood guard next to the original Victrola, represented the company's products for over 100 years. Like other companies which are responding to changing markets and products, RCA introduced Nipper's new partner. In a marketing effort to connect the past with the future the company has introduced the world to the puppy, Chipper. The puppy is, so to speak, a chip off the old block. Chipper represents the micro-chip and its potential for the future of entertainment products.

Chipper represents tomorrow's imagination.

Very few things have the staying power of Monopoly and Nipper. Everyone has heard the phrase "if it ain't broke don't fix it." In the changing environment of tomorrow if it ain't broke it **may be** near collapse. In the classic words attributable to the baseball pitcher Satchell Paige, "don't look back, someone might be gaining on you," describes the necessity. An updated version might say, "Don't look up they've already passed you."

The need to change and change often must become the benchmark capacity of modern organizations. Of all that changes, nothing is as fluid as the weather. Organizational capacity for change must be just as fluid. Management needs to appreciate what is so obvious in the weather. **Expect** no two days, two hours, or two minutes to be the same.

Historically, change has occurred slowly and predictably. Some change has even been short-sighted and unnecessary. The new context of change is **concerted**, **dynamic**, **simultaneous**, and **continuous**.

The Dutch Boy

Management has generally been reluctant to change. When things appeared to be going well organizations grew accustomed to the comfort of a predictable, stable operating environment. Yes, there have been **cosmetic** changes from time to time but wholesale change has never held prominence.

When organizational reluctance has been overcome, change has been approached in the one-dimensional style of the little Dutch boy who plugged holes in the dike one at a time. Each time he succeeded another hole sprang a leak. So goes the story of organizations. Management seems to have an uncanny ability to solve one problem and create another in the process.

Sputnik, Sauce, and Sedans

After Sputnik, education turned its emphasis to math and science. *The result?* American children forgot how to read and write. Then public policy directed education's attention back to basics. *The result?* A generation of children that couldn't compute and were scientifically illiterate.

In response to the nation's drinking problem, the U.S. Congress reluctantly passed the laws on prohibition (even though they chose not to provide any funding for enforcement). *The result?* The enactments created a criminal class that is still with us today and turned Treasury Department C.P.A.'s like Elliott Ness into famous G-Men. *The result?* First, creation of large federal agencies such as the F.B.I. and the Bureau of Alcohol, Tobacco, and Firearms to control the aforementioned criminal class. Second, repeal of prohibition!

After the 1973 oil embargo, the American auto industry was left with a large inventory of gas-guzzling cars. *The result?* The American consumer left Motown and started buying smaller, fuel efficient foreign imports. The U.S. auto makers followed the foreign competition and began building similar cars. *The result?* The oil crisis ended and demand for larger cars returned. *The result?* Automakers responded to the new demand. Then federal regulations and foreign competition changed the rules again. *The result?* Yogi Berra: "Dejavu all over again."

The incapacity to reach a balanced response to challenge seems to be a uniquely American problem. Responses to issues generally take a "push the pendulum in the other direction" behavior. For too many people, problems and responses are polarized as black and white and either or. It's like the person who is out in the cold, comes upon frozen gasoline and starts a fire to thaw it out. One problem just creates another! Each solution becomes a problem.

Change is an **action** term. It suggests movement, flexibility, and adaptability. Organizations and institutions have generally become so large and monolithic that they are little more than a set of undifferentiated, rigid parts that move more like a tortoise than a hare.

Managerial habits are so ingrained and unimaginative that they have led to irrational organizations which must stand by like a punch happy boxer and take the punishment. Punishment that is expensive and painful for the organization and its employees. Notice what downsizing has done to the unemployment lines?

It wasn't until foreign competitors began punching out American organizations in the canvass ring of competition that terms like **downsizing, flattening, realignment,** and **teams** were ever heard from management. Purposeful action has occurred as a last resort; more of a purposeful **reaction**.

Horizons

If only it were possible to see around the next corner, read the crystal ball, or know what was over the next horizon, change would be a simple matter. Statistical forecasting has certainly helped and realistic forecasts are readily available. Forecasting is not enough if what is sought is to know precisely what will happen next. Even though Toffler suggested there is greater coherence to the pattern, we do not know precisely what to expect next. The goal must be to facilitate enough flexibility and necessary preparation to allow all essential organizational units to "turn on a dime" (okay, maybe a dollar!).

Simultaneous change is the ability to change multiple parts at once. Modern organizations which desire to stand out from the crowd and create competitive advantage must stray from the usual course. Management must begin to exhibit aberrant behaviors which produce **innovation, risk-taking,** and **intrapreneurial** energy.

Innovations R Us

Innovations are everywhere. Microwave ovens, VCRs, automatic teller machines, answering machines, voice mail, lap top computers and fax machines are all recent innovations which **seem** like they have been around forever. The fact that they haven't illustrates how quickly technology is changing and how organizations must be constantly striving for market niche.

IBM has recently unveiled the wireless personal computer. The computer is about the length and width of a sheet of paper and weighs less than 6 1/2 lbs. The wireless allows computers to communicate with other computers through radio waves. This essentially eliminates the need for a regular telephone and modem, the latter a recent innovation itself. One model will even work through a cellular phone.

Eastman-Kodak began selling CD technology which can transfer pictures from film to compact discs. Once on the CD, images can be displayed on a TV screen or manipulated on a computer. Personal PCs with CD Rom are becoming commonplace.

Personal Financial Assistant, Inc. produced a new technology which allows banking by video. What an ATM is for the teller function, a PFA will duplicate for the service functions. A PFA is a 13 foot kiosk that operates like an automated teller machine.

Inside a booth similar to a teller cage, a customer can talk to a "banker" on a television screen any time of day or night. Customers can open a checking account, apply for a car loan, or access trust services by simply pushing a few buttons on an automatic dial phone. PFA's are available on 3 continents and in 17 languages. In addition to banking services, PFA's may have application to travel, real estate, and tax services as well.

One unique advantage of this system is that the banker cannot see the customer. Decisions on the customer's request is based on personal financial record, not appearance. Even though the banker on the screen is seen in "freeze-frame," 97% of customers in field tests believed they were dealing with a real person.

Innovation is caused by two converging necessities - market niche and customer satisfaction. Of course, it is important that each produces income too. Innovation means, let's improve.

The Ritz-Carlton in San Francisco puts disposable cameras in each guest's hotel room. This is a thoughtful response to those who leave on trips and forget their cameras. Like the alcoholic beverages provided in hotel rooms, the customer is only charged if the camera is used.

Toyota installed drivers-side airbags, knee protectors, and center mounted rear stoplights on its minivans.

Life Savers found something to do with their candy center. As a result Life Saver Holes was introduced as a separate product.

Fifty percent of the elevators sold in the next decade will not be installed in office buildings. Otis Elevator projects that one-half the elevators they sell will be placed in family residences.

In the near future pen-based computers will replace the keyboard. Palm top computer models will advance the standard PC. Imagine. The PC just celebrated its 10th anniversary in August of 1991 and palm size computers may soon render it obsolete!

Object-oriented software will hopefully re-invigorate the software industry before the end of the decade and VR (Virtual Reality) will permit individuals to enter computer generated worlds.

Not far behind are anti-aging chairs, eye-operated computers, voice credit cards, floating furniture, and the self-parking car.

Einstein said that imagination is more important than knowledge. He was right. So was George Orwell.

It's No Game

The board game *RISK* is designed to have opponents accumulate enough armies to occupy every territory on the board. The strategy is to determine the ideal time for players to **attack** their opponents and seize their territory. Most players wait until the size of their armies is sufficient enough to guarantee success.

The game makers provide an advantage for the players who risk their position and attack. Generally, those who wait for ideal circumstances end up losing. Those willing to take the risk usually prevail.

The board game has great similarity with the competitive realities of everyday management. Sometimes risk is not only necessary but **required**. Enjoying the comfort of present position only ensures that some other company will eventually assume the risk and attempt to seize market position.

Carpe Diem with a high cost.

Risk takes imagination. It takes guts. It means putting your neck on-the-line. Risk emulates the positive and productive qualities of small business. Risk-takers and the Maytag repairman have something in common. They are **both** lonely.

In many ways corporate culture defines risk. Some organizations encourage it; others do not. Some chief executives are willing to expose their companies to harm or loss even though the safest thing would be to travel a more conservative course.

- Federal Express made peanuts of the competition when it delivered (overnight) a 4 ton elephant named Tai to an Orlando, Florida movie set.
- Oracle may use the passing lane in a highly competitive race with software giant Microsoft.
- The movie Batman was produced and became a mega-hit even though the market research suggested it would flop.
- Frito-Lay capitalized on the apparent trend to light foods when it introduced its line of Cool Ranch Flavor chips.

- Federal Express was built on the idea that what UPS could do on the ground, they could do by air. One hundred thirty-five countries and 1.5 million plus delivered items a day later proves FederalExpress was right.
- Burger King's CEO turned a deaf ear to internal protests when he launched a broiled chicken sandwich without the usual market test. A million chicken sandwiches sold each day later proved him correct.
- Ford employees were given the power to shut down the assembly lines to design cars they would be willing to drive (after Ford lost $1.5 billion).
- Dell Computer Corporation ignored the naysayers when it expanded its mail order PC business into European markets. $240 million in European sales for the most recent fiscal year suggests the critics were wrong.

The UNcomfort Zone

The more often an organization tries to innovate and take risks, the more likely it is that **success** will be achieved.

Risk must escape the clutches of corporate bean counters. Risk is an on-going process that may fail more often than it succeeds. Failure is **the uncomfort zone** for corporate financial wizards who seek stability and predictability. What managers need is a synthesis of rationality and opportunistic resourcefulness.

The vast majority of organizations appear to be managed by individuals more interested in caution than risk. The doldrums that beset many organizations could be partially rectified if the **freedom for risk-taking** was encouraged and supported.

The Energizer

The idea of intrapreneurial energy suggests some changes inside the modern organization. It implies that management is looking away from traditional structures and processes to achieve results.

Organizations are using **coalitions** to work on special projects and activities and individual workers are being given more opportunity to work on ideas that interest them. The notion of coalitions suggests a collective energy to produce what can't be produced if individuals are working alone. Coalitions and individuals thrive in environments where failure is expected and tolerated.

A sort of organizational "born free."

The intrapreneurial spirit at 3M is marked by rules that keep employees from veering away from the company's bias toward creating new ideas. Turf fights, over-planning, and the "not invented here" syndrome are not permitted.

There is also the **15% rule**.

The 15% rule allows everyone at the company to spend up to 15% of their time on anything they want as long as it's project related. To support the 15% rule, 90 genius grants of $50,000 are awarded each year for new product development.

At Hewlett-Packard researchers are urged to spend 10% of their time on pet projects. The company keeps access to labs available 24 hours a day. It is this kind of opportunity that produced the laser jet printer. 60% of Hewlett-Packard's orders come from new products.

Johnson and Johnson built in the **freedom to fail** as a cultural prerogative. The company utilizes many autonomous working units to spur innovations.

Honeywell and Xerox help finance start-ups by employees who have promising ideas in return for a minority share.

SEI divides all its employees into intrapreneurial units. Each employee is given a 20% interest in their unit. After a suitable period an investment bank puts a price on the unit. Employees are then paid for their share.

The concept must be working. SEI recently ranked 53rd in its first appearance in the Fortune rankings of the best 200 small companies.

There are choices about how to combine people and technology. New corporate structures need to emphasize **innovation** over hierarchy and **gain sharing** over corporate gain.

Management should direct corporate energies toward highly focused sub-units operating by **self-supervision** and **empowerment**. Such arrangements might have profound influence on organizational effectiveness.

It is in the flexible workplace that the traditional win-win environment can be transformed into a 4-dimensional picture of success by making winners of customers, employees, shareholders, and employers.

In that order.

Death by Pin Prick

During the 1980s we were introduced to new Tide, new Coke, and NuSoft. New age thinking and new wave fashions are also part of the "new" family. Everything seems to be new and improved.

It is time for an additional change. Its time for change which produces innovation, risk, and intrapreneurial energy. New change components can be described as **concerted, simultaneous, continuous** and **dynamic**.

Herb Kellerher, Southwest Airlines' maverick CEO, presents it clearly. "When you have this tremendous flux in the outside world, you don't want to get fluxed yourself."

Organizations have tried the old model which featured one change at a time. It didn't work.

As a result, many of today's organizations are suffering death by pin prick.

11

The I-T-A Chain

"Nobody today can avoid technology."

What Work Requires of Schools
U.S. Department of Labor, 1991

As a native Detroiter, I looked forward to going every summer to grandma's house near Mayfield, Kentucky.

After the 600 mile drive, we would pull onto gravel and drive almost two miles on a narrow, winding road — then, there it was, turn to the right, up the incline through two rows of cedar trees to the brown-sided house where we would spend the next two weeks.

These summer occasions were so exciting that it never occurred to me that the surroundings were in any way sub par. The small farm house had no electricity so we used kerosene lamps. There was no running water so water was delivered and drawn from the cistern as it was needed.

There was no telephone. Grandpa's Model-T that went unutilized most of the time sat next to the cooling house. Often we would get in the mule-drawn wagon and ride the two miles to the store for supplies. The only part of it I recollect having any problem with was the outhouse. That seemed a little barbarian to my twelve year old mind, but the rest of the adventure, excitement, and quaintness of our annual visit was wonderful.

In retrospect, no way could you consider Grandma's house high tech!

By city standards, somebody had screwed up!

Progress as we know it is made possible by a three-pronged chain reaction involving **idea, technology,** and **application**.

Idea

Back in 1983, people living in Chicago swallowed cyanide contaminated Tylenol. Johnson and Johnson, the makers of the nation's top selling headache remedy, reacted promptly. They recalled and destroyed more than 30 million pills and capsules. Many people felt that the brand name would have no future whatsoever, but the Tylenol management had an idea. They decided to continue Tylenol with a new safety device: a tamper-resistant seal. The new packaging saved Tylenol, and has been applied broadly by many other makers of numerous other products.

At least one idea has built a city: Detroit. The idea was the wheel, but it wasn't conceived in the motor city. The wheel can be traced back to 3500 B.C. The spoked wheel did not appear until 2000 B.C. And people have been "reinventing" the wheel for new uses ever since. Robert Fulton had to conceive of the steamboat; Eli Whitney had to conceptualize the cotton gin. Occasionally, an idea presents itself by accident such as when vulcanized rubber was discovered.

1991 was the 150th anniversary of the tube. A relatively unknown

19th century artist, John Goffe Rand, wanted to take his painter's palette outside. Since then the tube has had an infinite number of uses. Even with today's alternate dispensers, Americans maintain their crush on the toothpaste tube.

Invention anniversaries abound in the 1990s. Kool-Aid was 60, peanut butter 100, and Orville Redenbacher's popcorn celebrated its silver anniversary.

New ideas are ubiquitous. MCC, the U.S.A.'s top microelectronics and computer consortium, has applied for 54 patents in a four-year time period. One of their idea breakthroughs is a tiny low-power amplifier that will boost superconducting voltage levels.

Desktop publishing is only one generation old. And today computer minds are experimenting with such new concepts as "virtual reality." Cyberspace, the next frontier, awaits new innovations.

Idea innovation knows no age boundary.

In June 1991 the Invent America competition selected some young minds at work for awards. First grader, Elizabeth Hay of Edgewood, Pennsylvania, won first place for her idea of putting grabbing tabs on plastic wrap. Second grader, Benjamin Christgau, came up with the idea of parking meters that accepted credit cards. Fifth grader, B.J. Baker, thought how convenient it would be to put twine and a staple gun in one operation. Finally, seventh grader, Sara Blumer, conceived of touch-tone voting.

Technology

In 1970 Alvin Toffler divided the entire history of the human race (50,000 years) into 800 lifetimes of 62 years each. He observed that communication from one life to another had only been possible for 70 lifetimes, mass print for 6, accurate time measure for 4 generations, the electric motor for only 2. His most startling observation was that the vast majority of all the material goods have been made in **our present** life time.

Toffler's theme in 1970 was that change was going to occur even faster in the future and he was right. Only 13 years later in 1983, *Time* magazine named the computer as its machine-of-the-year instead of its normal person-of-the-year cover story.

In 1992, 98% of American homes had television, 93% had telephones, 72% had VCRs, and more than one-half million people had a pace maker. There were 2.6 million personal computers in American homes in 1985. By 1995 there will be 9 million.

E-mail has become a common practice in business offices. Instead of dictation, typing, copying, sorting, and distributing via paper, the new process allows direct typing on a computer and punching a code that sends the memos to locations all over the country or the world. A decade ago less than one-half million people used electronic mail. By the early 1990s, more than 12 million of us were dancing the E-Mail Boogie.

Computer technology is still hot and happening. In August 1991 IBM showcased a new wireless personal computer. The machine weighs less than seven pounds and is no larger than a standard size sheet of paper.

One major new breakthrough is computers that utilize the human language, *Space Odyssey* style. In the early 1980s such computers were large mainframes with limited vocabulary of 5,000 words. Utilization was limited by voice recognition variation in accent and individual users had to spend hours working with the computer for accurate voice recognition.

Ten years later a great deal of progress has been made. By 1991 voice recognition systems have been transferred to personal computers with vocabularies as high as 30,000 words. Today's talk is also cheaper. In the mid 80s speech recognition capability would have cost as much as $90,000. Now some of the better models are available for $5,000.

Only a few years back, "just the facts" would have been easily recognized as a Jack Webb line in the television show, *Dragnet.* But in the 1990s the meaning and the spelling are different.

In the late 1960s, Xerox and Magnavox were ready to spend a great deal of money in developing the fax machine. Twenty two years ago only 4,000 were being used. They may have been a bit ahead of the technology. Twenty-six years ago it took an entire day to send a dozen regular size sheets.

By 1987 the price was down and performance was up. Three thousand units were sold in that one year. Today, the fax is ubiquitous.

Technology has also been important in many other areas including safety. Most of you will remember the infamous wind-shear crash in Dallas in 1985. The response was a new technology: **anemometers**.

You'll be glad to know that not one airline death since that 1985 crash has been attributed to abrupt shifts in wind speed. That is quite a statement considering that almost 600 people died between 1970 and 1985 in wind-shear related crashes. In the past 16 years 110 airports have acquired anemometers (a wind-shear alert mechanism).

Other examples of technological breakthroughs or improvements abound. But America's problem rests mostly with **application**.

Application

When it comes to utilizing what we think up with technology that is already in existence, America has an **application gap**. The Council on Competitiveness report in the spring of 1991 would argue more of a **hiatus**! The Council graded American performance in most major technologies and concluded that we were weak in more than one-third of the categories. Ten years earlier we would have been a strong competitor in virtually **all** of them.

The specific problem pinpointed was turning what we knew into actual products or services. It took us 20 years to develop the microwave. Horizontal drilling didn't catch on until a decade or more past the oil embargo of 1973. Our K-12 educational classroom would still be very recognizable to Rip Van Winkle.

As a matter of fact Rip would be quite **comfortable** in the American **higher** education classroom.

IBM Vice President of Academic Information Systems, L. G. Waterhouse, was recently asked on a scale of one to ten how he would rank college utilization of instructional technology. His reply: "1 or 2." And that observation gets strong support from Robert Atwell, president of the American Council on Education. In March of 1991 he told educators in Orlando, Florida that higher education simply "had not taken advantage of technology in the classroom."

To be fair, some significant application efforts are going on. Vanderbilt University has designed a cutting-edge electronic classroom. It allows computer and audiovisual technology to be mixed so that film, videos, graphics, and text can be utilized simultaneously. Michigan State University is utilizing Dragon Dictate, which allows handicapped students to run a computer by voice. More than one hundred of the nation's three thousand plus colleges and universities have installed registration by phone technology. The League for

Innovation, an association of some 15 community colleges, has undertaken a project called Synergy. EDUCOM has identified 101 examples of technology that is being used in the nation's classrooms.

These efforts are encouraging, but they still are too few, untimely, and drastically behind the need curve.

One brilliant business effort recognizing the need to get from idea to technology to application is Sematech. Based in Austin, Texas Sematech aims to increase U.S. competitiveness in manufacturing. Recently, W.J. Spencer, president of Sematech, announced semiconductor breakthroughs that would provide a potential 75% increase in manufacturing capacity.

But application does not have to be in manufacturing or education.

Giant Foods has been the innovator of many new applications in the grocery business. Giant concentrates on low prices by cutting out the middle man. It produces some of its own brands, does its own advertising, and even builds some of the shopping centers where it is located. CEO Israel Cohen, from his Landover, Maryland home office, has taken Giant to much larger application advantages than his competitors. In 1990 Giant's profit margin was more than double that of his competitors.

Even **government** is trying to fill the application gap. The Wayne County Circuit Court in Detroit keeps the records of some trial proceedings via video tape rather than court reporter. Michigan is one of seventeen states and more than 130 courts in the U.S.A. that allows video court reporters. The Wayne County Court believes that the video system is more efficient and 100% accurate. Court administrator, Terry Kuykendall, believes that the system will save $300,000 per court room over an eight-year period when compared with a full-time employee.

None the less, the **gaposis** malady remains. Why?

Efforts to close the **idea, technology, application** chain are impacted by five major factors: cost, risk, real need, governmental incentive, and competition.

Cost is always a consideration because completing the loop will be worthless without a consumer. High definition television is a case in point. The Federal Communications Commission is now in the process of testing six systems for high definition television. Expected to be available between 1995 and 2000, the improved technology would cost up to **ten times** today's television receivers.

The second factor is fear of failure. Many managers would rather sit on the sidelines and wait until the **risk** is lower. Thirty years ago both Armour and Swift were strongly attracted to the idea of dehydrated meat. They spent a bundle of money aiming to eliminate the need for refrigeration. Dehydration had a couple of problems for the American public: it didn't taste very good and the elimination of refrigeration was primarily a benefit for Armour and Swift. Thirty years later the failure is evident. About the only dehydrated meat you can find is beef jerky.

Real need is a major force, which sometimes overcomes cost and risk.

In the summer of 1991, Mission Industries opened a new $2.5 million high-tech laundry. Although, it isn't something that would be needed in many cities across the country, it is needed in Austin, Texas where high tech has become a large and growing concern. The plant is state of the art utilizing deionized water, stainless steel machinery, and other special features such as a chamber where impurities can be tested. Certified as a class-one laundry, Mission Industries can allow no more than 36 particles per cubic foot.

A second need-based application is governmental: the Internal Revenue Service. Believe it or not, the IRS is becoming more user friendly. After years of dealing with an avalanche of paper, the IRS is testing several alternatives. Effective in January 1992 Ohio taxpayers could file by phone. The process takes less than ten minutes and allows refunds within a month. In several other states the IRS allows about 300,000 to file Form EZ-1. The IRS takes the answers to three questions and does all the mathematical computations. IRS has already invited tax returns via personal computers, utilizing a 1040PC approach. Ten million people utilized such electronic options in 1992.

Another example of real need as the driving force comes from automobile painting. Remember how angry you were when your silver Ford over oxidized or your beautiful red Cadillac faded under the summer sun? Maybe the salt rusted out your rocker panels or everything that touched your car seemed to chip the paint. No **more**.

The technology for preventing all of the above situations has been thought up, figured out, and applied.

John Young, an executive engineer for Ford, explains the rather complicated process. It begins with two-sided galvanized steel that is cleaned and coated with a special phosphate and then dipped. A primer coat is applied inside and outside. The exterior is given another coat of primer, a base coat, and another clear coat to protect its exterior finish. Today's Arcadia Green and Jadestone hot colors are quite durable.

A fourth factor that can have strong influence on completing the I-T-A chain is **governmental incentive**. Two current examples are automobile emissions and airplane noise.

As it so often does, California leads the nation in auto emission requirements. Its new law requires that 5% of the cars sold in California will be non-polluting by the year 2000. Several other states including the Northeast Ozone Transport Commission (a twelve-state consortium) are moving in that direction and standards for emission in Europe and Japan are on the same track. No surprise then with **zero emission** legislation that there is a renewed interest in electric cars that don't pollute.

In early 1991 General Motors announced its new Impact would be produced in Lansing, Michigan. Without the California and Federal legislation that forces auto manufacturers to adopt at least the 1990 Federal Clean Act standards, the battery operated Impact would go the way of former electric car promoters. But with the governmental push GM is taking the plunge.

With its new Impact, GM has made breakthroughs in aerodynamics and tires, but speed and range are still problematical. The government incentive, however, included a four-year $130 million Federal subsidy to help develop light weight batteries for the new electric cars.

The second governmental incentive push comes from the Federal Aviation Administration via its requirements for cutting noise at airports.

The FAA policy requires all airlines to eliminate the noisiest planes in their possession by the year 2000. The get-tough policy will take about 2,300 stage-two airplanes (over half of the existing domestic total) out of service.

The fifth I-T-A chain motivator is **competition**. If you doubt that, just talk with Robert Weisshappel at Motorola. Weisshappel headed a Motorola team at the Pan American Cellular Subscriber Group that developed the first palm-size cellular telephone.

Today's competition is tough and it is going to get tougher.

A return visit to grandmother's house in 1995 would be eye opening. It's all there **now**. But the progress the I-T-A chain must make in the next half decade means nothing less than our economic survival.

12

Popcorn

"American managers need to put away their hunches, guesses, intuition, power trips, and posturing. Until these tinker toys are put back in the can, American quality will stay there."

Mike DeVault

In 1957 when I graduated from Michigan's East Detroit High School, the phrase "made in Japan" meant souvenir items, creative paper goods, and poor quality.

Times have changed

The beginning of the change can be traced back 45 years. In 1950, Eiji Toyota visited Detroit to study how vehicles were made. His firm had made less than 3,000 automobiles in a dozen years compared to the 7,000 that Ford's River Rouge plant was turning out each day. Toyota made his study and returned to Japan impressed but not bewildered. He informed his associates in Japan that some

improvements could be made.

The next 20 years were largely catch up, but there were deep conceptual changes taking place while the numbers were becoming reasonably similar. And during the 70s the Japanese quality emphasis (led by United States consultant Edwards Deming) became clearly visible. So visible, in fact, that by 1980 Ford decided to **return the trip** to see how it was done in Japan.

During the 1980s several manufacturers and a few service businesses decided they were doing something wrong. They had ample evidence.

Metalloy, a 50 year old metal casting company in Hudson, Michigan had been a long-term supplier for GM, Ford, and Chrysler for many years. When they were contacted by NOK, a large Japanese parts supplier, they enthusiastically accepted the contract and soon shipped 5,000 rubber rings to be inserted in metal casings.

To Metalloy's surprise, they were soon notified that there were **15 defective parts** among the first batch of 5,000. NOK was **very** upset. Metalloy President David Berlin felt that 15 out of 5,000 "was pretty good." He was surprised at the chewing out he got.

That single instance with Metalloy says volumes about how the United States has regarded **quality** throughout its manufacturing heyday. The mass production system called for a large enough number of widgets to toss out a certain percentage. Rejects could be reworked or become permanent scrap. It didn't matter that the scrap items cost a lot or that additional workers had to be involved to inspect and repair a large number of duds.

No surprise then, with this mentality, that 20¢ of each $1 spent in American business goes into rework and scrap, that up to one-forth of our employees don't add value to or produce anything, or that consumers world-wide rank our products considerably below their own and those of other countries.

Although quality by all measures has been becoming more and more important for the last 20 years, a dramatic difference can be found between 1978 and 1990. Twelve years ago 30% of our population felt that quality was more important than price. As the decade of the 1990s began the number has almost **tripled**!

Recently one of my colleagues said that he had read about a national Quality Forum and that he was surprised to learn that it was the tenth such forum. He was totally unaware of forums one through nine. He is not in the minority. Thousands of managers throughout the country in manufacturing, services, education, and government have paid no heed either.

James B. Hays, publisher of *Fortune* magazine kicked off Quality Forum Seven in New York on October 1, 1991. The event was broadcast via satellite to more than 100,000 business leaders all over the world.

Former IBM chairman, John Akers, told how IBM had been curtailing errors, that defects were being eliminated three times faster than in earlier years, and that the new goal of IBM was less than 4 defects per 1,000,000 parts by 1994.

General Motors chairman, Robert Stempel, challenged viewers to try to find the difference between cars in Japan and the highest quality cars built in the U.S.A.

Ray Groves, chairman of Ernst and Young, reported on a two-year international quality study involving 500 businesses in Canada, Germany, Japan, and the United States. The study was encouraging for the U.S.A. indicating that quality perceptions of U.S.A. products were **improving**. Unfortunately, we still have a **considerable** distance to go.

Although the strongest motivation for a renewed quality emphasis comes from external competition and the result of necessity to stay alive, **believe it or not**, some of the new awareness of quality has come about as a result of the U.S. government.

In 1987 Congress passed the Malcolm Baldrige Quality Improvement Act. The intent was to promote an awareness of quality, to recognize quality achievements, and to publicize quality leaders by awarding a national Baldrige Quality Award to manufacturing companies, service companies, and small businesses.

The first awards were given in 1988, and over the past 7 years 22 companies or divisions of large companies have been chosen: 1988: Motorola Inc., Westinghouse Commercial Nuclear Fuel Division, Globe Metallurgical, Inc.; 1989: Milliken & Co., Xerox Corp.; 1990: Cadillac Motor Car Division, GM, IBM, Federal Express, Wallace Co.; 1991: Solectron Corp., Zytec Corp., Marlow Industries (Dallas); 1992: AT&T Network Systems Group, Texas Instruments Inc., AT&T Universal Card Services, Ritz-Carlton Hotel Co., Granite Rock Co.; 1993: Eastman Chemical Co., Ames Rubber Corp.; 1994: AT&T Consumer Communications Services, GTE Directories Corp., and Wainwright Industries, Inc.

The Baldrige Award is based on seven criteria and the word quality is directly or indirectly applied in all seven yardsticks. It was intended to do for the U.S.A. what the Deming Award did for the Japanese.

In the spring of 1992 *USA Today* and the Rochester Institute of Technology awarded a new national quality award, the Quality Cup. The award goes beyond the Baldrige focus of quality improvement by **divisions** or entire **companies**. The goal is to honor **teams** and **individuals** who are involved in quality goods and services. There are also a number of new city, county, and community awards modeled after the Baldrige Quality Cup examples.

Has any of this new focus on quality made a difference?

Yes, according to at least one poll. In the early 1990s, Brouillard Communications reported that more than 50% of American adults felt that the United States now **leads** Japan and Germany in high-quality products. Unfortunately, we do not rank that high or compare so well in other parts of the world.

There is no doubt, however, that we have made some strong strides in the last few years. Some of our national improvement is due to efforts of firms like Motorola that discovered that George Orwell's *1984* could have been a fair warning to their enterprise.

In the early 1980s Motorola was in big trouble in the world market place. Putting the matter simply, their quality was not up to snuff.

Among a number of changes to the corporate culture, Motorola locked on the concept of **Six Sigma**. Their aim was **quantitative quality improvement**. Six Sigma is a statistical term that has to do with standard deviation. Throughout the 1970s and 80s U.S. manufacturers had been very willing to live with "good" or "good enough." Motorola managers gazed into the mirror and asked the question, "Mirror, mirror on the wall who has the best quality of all?" They were treated like the wicked witch in Snow White. They felt like they'd had a bite of the poison apple.

In world quality terms, what Motorola **had been** putting out was 95% plus quality. The new criteria would be the Sixth Sigma quality, 99.9997% perfection (only 3.4 defects per 1,000,000 products).

Six Sigma was a measuring device created in response to quality statistical efforts started in Japan many years earlier. Japan had started using SPC (Statistical Process Controls) in the 1950s.

In the 1970s the Japanese had introduced a new tool: DOE (Design of Experimentation). DOE was a highly sophisticated statistical means to establish a 100% **cause and effect** relationship between variation problems discovered (illness) and specific solutions eliminating variations (cure).

Even in the 1990s the DOE method is relatively unknown and rarely used in America. That is strange indeed, since the concept was invented in the United States many years before it was applied in Japan.

DOE is based on the same principle of American agricultural efforts to discover the best frequency, fertilizer, planting methods, seed derivatives, and crop rotations that would provide the maximum yield. Although our agricultural produce has been the wonder of the world, we made no effort to apply this technique to manufacturing and product quality.

Some of our inability to apply the agricultural DOE concept comes from our lock-step mass manufacturing mentality. In manufacturing automobiles, for example, the goal is to do a quick fix via **tinkering** and keep the assembly line moving. Although the assembly line rolls, the problem will almost always reoccur because the exact cause was never discovered — maybe it was the temperature, maybe it was the steel, maybe it was the design. **Maybe** is the exact opposite of DOE.

Some feel that DOE is too complicated because it relies on sophisticated statistical terms such as evolutionary optimization and orthogonal arrays. Yet, the principle is simple and it's our own invention.

Thomas Charette, has come up with an easy, crystal clear explanation of DOE: **popcorn**.

Charette paints a scene of a family argument concerning the best way to make popcorn. Differing family members propose the method they think best: hot air, open flame, microwave, or the purchase of gourmet products. With this kitchen scenario, we can all approach quality by aiming at getting all kernels to pop. Which solution will the family members accept? Will it be decided on the basis of who shouts the loudest? Head of household authority? Or some other more irrational factor?

According to DOE, we need to design an experiment to determine which of the variables results in more kernels popping **each and every time**. When that is done, we have located the cause and the effect. DOE is experimentation with variables to determine a cause and effect relationship from any variance discovered.

American managers need to put away their hunches, guesses, intuition, power trips, and posturing. Until these tinker toys are put back in the can, American quality will stay there.

DOE is very powerful and it is a tremendous step in the right direction. It allows us to lose the variance acceptance inspection mindset of the past and to move toward **perfection** in popping all of our kernels, batch after batch.

What do we **really** mean by quality? Fancy features? Clean design? Flashy styling? Something that works well? Something that works most of the time?

In general, quality exists when high standards exist for performance, reliability, and durability. It is a far cry from the U.S.A. of the early post-war years and will require nothing short of a **new culture** design and implementation in manufacturing, services, education, and governmental effort at the local, state, and national level. Some of that change in corporate culture can be seen at Whistler Manufacturing in Massachusetts.

Whistler is a manufacturer of radar detectors. Nine years ago one out of every four radar detectors was failing inspection. Some of the defects were not repairable and one of their two plants had more than $2 million of defective inventory piled up against the wall. One hundred of their two hundred and fifty workers were spending their time trying to fix defective pieces.

Management instituted major cultural change and quality improved drastically. In two years the defect rate went from 25% to 1%! Their quest for quality is still going forward.

Pennsylvania's Corning Glass faced their quality demons close up and one-on-one in 1983. A truck pulled up at their State College location from another Corning Glass factory that had just closed. The workers and management knew that they had one year, maybe two, to drastically improve their quality.

With a renewed quality focus, born out of necessity, Corning aimed at significantly racheting up their quality.

In 1983 customers returned 4 of every 100 pieces because of defects.

Instituting a number of quality improvements, including examination under a bright florescent light, Corning started to correct these defects **before** they left the plant. Within five years they were able to reduce the 4 in 100 returns to 3 in 1,000.

A concern and focus on quality is not the lone property of manufacturers. Quality is and should be a major part of **service** in the 1990s. Did you get your bags when you last traveled on an airline? How long is your check-out counter wait? Did your car get fixed properly the **first** time you took it in?

Quality can also be demonstrated at the governmental level. Look at Madison, Wisconsin.

Starting in 1983 under the leadership of Mayor Joseph Sensenbernner, Madison wrestled with the need to do more with less. Their solution was a series of quality initiatives that resulted in more bang for the buck: police officer shift transfers were handled with an improved information technique that saved 800 hours of overtime pay; city workers found they were able to reduce an eight-step purchasing process to only three steps; garbage truck employees studied their workplace and successfully reduced time lost due to injuries. Sensenbernner feels that such measures could eliminate more than **10%** of local government costs.

No doubt about it, "Let the buyer beware" is bunk in the world of the 1990s.

The quality breakthrough has occurred in Japan. It is arriving in other parts of the world and has taken a strong toe-hold in leading manufacturing and service businesses in the United States. The quality breakthrough will revive, reinvigorate, and renew hundreds or even thousands of business enterprises.

The question is, will **yours** be one of them?

13

Surprise and Delight

*"All but a few managers are blind to
the growing demand for service."*

William H. Davidow
Total Customer Service

In October 1991 United Flight 714 had just finished boarding. An elderly man wanted to go the rest room. He made his way toward the rear of the plane where he found a rather rude reception. The flight attendant standing in the middle of isle said rather sharply, "No. You will have to go back, we are just about ready to push off."

There was no "Sorry," just her staccato statement of impending departure. The elderly man complied rather docilely and went back to his seat. The plane took off all right—**20 minutes later!**

A Midwest CEO arrived midday at Washington state's Seatac Airport. Her bags arrived quickly and she was delighted to see that it was a beautiful autumn day as she caught the very prompt Alamo shuttle that took her to the car rental station. Soon she discovered a drastic hitch in rent-a-car proceedings.

As the bus pulled into the lot, she observed several people standing in line **outside**. There also were people standing in line **inside**. And there were more people standing in line **at** the check-out counter.

"Unbelievable," she exclaimed, as she witnessed more than 100 people waiting to check out a car. About one and one-half hours later she negotiated the process and left with her automobile. **Nobody** apologized for the delay. **Nobody** offered her an upgrade. As a matter of fact she thought she was waited on by **Nobody**.

"What a wonderful Hawaiian vacation," the Angel family thought as they returned home from their two-week Christmas holiday. The beaches had been warm, new friendships had been formed, and fond memories of Hawaii would forever linger in their thoughts.

They didn't linger very long!

Within two weeks a bill arrived from Kanola at Kona saying that the Angels owed for the evenings of December 21 and 22. The problem was that on these two evenings the Angels had stayed at another hotel. Mr. Angel was steamed and wrote a rather warm letter to the management. Mrs. Angel contacted the customer service branch of Citibank. It took about three weeks, but Citibank finally resolved the issue.

Three moments of truth.
On a scale of one to ten United, Alamo, and the Kanola at Kona customer satisfaction quotient didn't even register on the scale.

A **moment of truth** occurs when a product or service comes in contact with a customer. Karl Albrecht and Ron Zemke define a moment of truth as "an episode in which a customer comes in contact with any aspect of the company and has an opportunity for an impression."

There are millions of such opportunities for success or failure in each business day.

How are we doing?

Poor. Shoddy. Bad. Sloppy. Awful. Rife with snafus. Glitch prone. Robotized. Getting worse.

As a matter of fact, consumer frustration is reaching new heights.

Gullible Labeling

With 80,000 types of food and 300,000 food brands, consumers, according to David Kessler, Commission of the Food and Drug Administration, are hungry for information they can trust and understand. On November 7, 1991 the F&D Administration issued the most significant regulations for food labeling since WWII.

Coming from massive shopper dismay, frustration, and hypertension caused by nonsensical food package labeling, the new rules provide a uniform set of labels to describe vocabulary attached to various products. "Sodium-free, salt-free" now means less than 5mg of sodium per serving. "Low-fat" means no more than 3g per 100g of food.

Why did the government step in? Because of the massive dissatisfaction by America's 250 million consumers.

Other frustrations are easily identifiable.

Just reach into your back pocket or purse, pull out any one of the plastic cards and prepare to go **bonkers**.

In the past few years the interest rate on a twelve-month certificate of deposit has dropped from more than 8% to less than **5%**. But the average rate on a credit card has **risen** to almost **19%**. Congressman Charles Schumer (Democrat), New York, understates the situation when he says, "The public is fed up with these high rates."

Monotone Mania

One of the most exasperating and recent abuses of the customer comes via telephone sales **from a machine**. This phenomena has gotten steadily worse as the technology becomes cheaper.

In early 1992 some twenty million people were hassled each day by telemarketers.

Things had gotten so far out of hand that in 1991 Senator Ernest Hollings (Democrat), South Carolina, convinced the Senate to stamp out this blight. Hollings refers to telemarketers using auto-dialing machines as "the scourge of the civilized world" and he wants to get customer permission before such calls can be made. A recent Roper Poll reported that three out of four respondents found such practices "extremely annoying."

What makes all of these instances doubly perplexing is that America is becoming more and more a service economy. We started down that road back in 1956, the first year American workers numbered more in white-collars than blue-collars. Over the past forty years, we have shifted to a ratio of more than three white-collars to one blue.

Today more than 60% of our workforce provides **service** rather than **product**. By the end of the century nearly **nine** out of every **ten** American workers will earn their living via service.

It stands to reason then that service must get better.

Oddly enough, we know far more about what to do than we have been willing to deliver.

A composite of recent knowledge concerning customer satisfaction would yield this significant eight-point profile:

1. 2% of the complainers **can't** be satiated
2. Only 3% of customers actually **complain**
3. 90% of those dissatisfied don't complain, they **walk**
4. One unhappy customer will **tell** 10 others
5. Each complaint **represents** 25
6. A satisfied customer will **tell** 5 others
7. 7 out of 10 customers who **switch** do it because of poor service
8. It **costs** much more to find new customers than it does to keep current customers

The moral of the story? Modern-day America is not a field of dreams. If you build it, they may come. But, if your service is shabby, they won't stay! As only Yogi Berra could capture it, "If people don't want to come out to the ballpark, nobody's gonna stop 'em."

What is different about customers in the 90s than in the past?

Plenty.

Today's customers are more sophisticated, keenly aware of the competition, have come to expect great variety, have heightened expectations, and have very little brand loyalty.

Who's Hot?

When it comes to beating the tar out of the competition, Atlanta based Home Depot is hotter than Georgia asphalt.

Home Depot caters to the do-it-yourself segment of the home remodeling market. You pick the tool and Home Depot is the pile driving winner. Annual growth rate? Eight inch to one inch. Sales in existing stores? Eight penny to two penny?

How do they do it?

Customer service is the lynch pin. Home Depot aims to make a real Mr. or Mrs. Fix-it out of the novices who come calling. Company stores are staffed by knowledgeable salespeople. Most stores have a licensed electrician and workshops are frequently held to show customers how to do various do-it-yourself tasks. Home Depot also stocks more than three times the competitor's inventory for customer convenience.

When a Home Depot store produces sales which surpass $400 per square foot, the company is likely to close it. Why? The store is probably too crowded. In order to improve the shopping experience of customers, Home Depot may open two smaller stores to replace the one they closed. Customer service is the logical extension of customer attention. At Home Depot, customers get both.

Over a seven year period, its 50 stores multiplied to 175. The company wants to increase the number of its stores by 25% per year. Thirty new stores will open this year and there will be more than 500 by 1996.

Another national chain wagering heavily on the customer service horse to win (not place or show) is 7-Eleven with 6,600 stores scattered throughout Canada and the U.S. 7-Eleven is **piloting** some major facelifting.

Based upon customer research, West Hargrove, a test market manger has **lowered** prices on basic items to be more competitive, changed the store's image by removing video games and clutter, and added 400 or so new items including fresh fruit and vegetables and microwave fare. Hargrove says that by **listening** to customer wants, 7-Eleven is taking actions that will be necessary by everybody who is to be successful in the 1990s.

Irregularity

Airline complaints reached an all-time high in 1987 after deregulation. There were mergers, massive schedule changes, and general disruption in flight arrangements.

A recent report by the Department of Transportation Consumer Affairs Office said that things **have gotten better** in the last few years. More flights are landing within 15 minutes of posted times, baggage complaints are down, and fewer passengers are being bumped by over bookings. The most dramatic change was in time of arrival. Among the big three carriers, Delta had gone from 72% to 86%, United went from 79% to 87%, and American from 84% to 86%. The problem of lost or damaged baggage affected only 4 passengers per 1,000 in 1991. A year earlier it was almost 6 per 1,000.

Going the Extra Mile

Customer service basically means treating customers as a friend rather than a stranger, extending common courtesies, and acting in a humanitarian way. In the 1990s it means going the extra mile.

Monica Simms made a business trip to Atlanta and stayed at the Radisson Hotel. After she checked out of her room, she discovered she had misplaced her plane ticket.

Much to her delight the Radisson staff had not only found her ticket amongst the hotel trash, but actually had it delivered to the airport in time for her to catch her plane.

Ame Gorena took a consulting trip to Montana. Having misplaced her plane ticket, she dialed her air carrier and was told that she would have to purchase a new full-fare ticket. This was quite a problem since she had also lost her cash and credit cards.

Next she dialed her Carlson Travel Network hotline. Much to her surprise she soon learned that not only would there be a return ticket waiting at Helena, but the ticket would be issued at the regular government discount rate. She breathed a huge sigh of relief. The Carlson Travel Network would have a loyal customer.

Compaq Computer Corporation recently unveiled 100 new desktop computers and cut prices on existing models. This Texas-size commitment to customer satisfaction was a big surprise and a pleasant delight.

Such stories could go on and on, but the point is clear—customer service, be it via a manufacturer, service agency, an educational institution, or a government entity, has become absolutely essential. Customer expectations have been on a steady pattern of ascension and the high bar is going to be raised.

A consumer revolt

The U.S. Post Office is no longer going to be able to announce that it delivers 97% of its Express Mail promptly and on time the next day. The Post Office can satisfy only 65% of the public in Chicago, 72% in Queens, and 75% in Los Angeles.

The erratic, secretive, and irritating habits of credit reporting services will have to change drastically. In 1990 the Federal Trade Commission experienced 9,000 complaints. Of the nine million Americans who requested copies of their credit reports, **one in three** found errors.

Two conclusions can be drawn rather readily from the lack of outstanding and stellar customer service: (1) the U.S.A. has been too **product** driven in the past, and (2) American manufacturers, service firms, governmental entities, and educational institutions have been too **internally** directed.

In the last decade of the 20th century, we will not be able to deliver service that only meets an acceptable level of expectation. We will need to go beyond that and provide a little bit more. Today's customers know good service when they don't get it.

In the 1990s whatever your contact with the customer, the aim is going to have to be to **surprise** and **delight**!

14

Poof

"I have only just a minute,
Only sixty seconds in it,
Forced upon me—can't refuse it
Didn't seek it, didn't choose it,

But it's up to me to use it.
I must suffer if I lose it,
Give account if I abuse it.
Just a tiny little minute—
But eternity is in it!"

—Author Unknown

In September 1991 a startling event took place in the world of comics. Dean Young, the artist who sketches the well-known comic strip *Blondie*, said that a major change would take place in his cartoon strip. Blondie Bumstead, the beloved wife of Dagwood and mother of Alexander and Cookie, was going to enter into the world of work.

The column that began in 1930 was created by Chic Young, Dean's father. And although the majority of this generation might not realize it, the cartoon strip underwent major surgery during its first three years.

Originally, Dagwood was a rich playboy who was pursuing Blondie even though his parents disapproved. When the depression hit, Blondie and Dagwood got married and began to mirror many of the daily problems reflected in struggling middle-class Americans.

If the strip responded to the depression era need so quickly, why did it take so long to respond to the reality of the working woman and the two-paycheck family? It certainly isn't something that happened in the last year or so. In the 1990s more than 70% of the women between the ages of 20 and 53 work. Almost 50% of women over 16 were in the workforce in October 1991. In 1992 there were 56 million working women who composed 45% of the total workforce.

This major trend of the last 20 plus years has had a massive impact on our society. But no where has the impact been greater than the new demand for **speed**.

According to pollster Louis Harris, the amount of leisure time of an average American has shrunk by more than 30% over the last two decades. At the same time the average work week jumped from 40 to 47 hours. Many vocations require a 60- to an 80-hour workweek.

Tortoises

In a world focused on speed a number of companies remain unaware of the 4.88 second drag racing record established by Gary Ormsby in 1990. The majority are still contemplating the 5.97 record set by Mike Sinvely in 1972. And several are back with Jack Chrisman's 8.97 mark of 30 years ago.

In the early 90s, the Congressional Budget Office came up with a new definition of the S&L crisis. Instead of savings and loan, the meaning seemed to be **sickening** and **loathing**. The CBO reported that regulators hadn't closed S&Ls until they had been insolvent for more than a year and a half. There seemed to be endless delays with bureaucrats that were frightened to death of making a decision on what to sell and when. The delay in closing more than 1,100 ailing thrifts between 1980 and 1990 cost the American public **$66 billion**.

No question about it, the large insurance rating agencies reacted far too slowly in alerting policy holders of impending insurance failures in 1991. When Mutual Benefit Life Insurance was taken over by New Jersey regulators in mid July 1991, Moody more or less admitted its past slow action by lowering the ratings of six big insurers **within a week after** the July 16 takeover.

Harley-Davidson has experienced a major turn around in the last seven years. With motorcycle sales providing more than two-thirds of company revenue, they have been unable or unwilling to meet additional demands. "They can't run their production line fast enough to keep up with supply," said one industry analyst.

In October 1991 the Soviet Union made no secret of the fact that it was seeking **fast** help, which wasn't going to be possible from large U.S. companies. Sergey Chetverikov, a high ranking diplomat at the Soviet Washington Embassy, said that a company like Chevron might make a major investment but it would take "so many years." While some large companies were deciding whether or not to invest in the new Soviet economy, Biomet Inc. of Warsaw, Indiana chalked up $2 million in sales to the Soviets in 1990.

Education has also been extremely slow in reacting to modern-day needs. *A Nation at Risk*, a well-known document calling for massive reform, was issued in 1983.

Twelve years later we have made little progress.

Nowhere is the lack of Road Runner's speed more apparent than looking at the nation's former largest retailer: Sears.

"Sufferin' succotash," you might well exclaim.

As other recognizable department stores, such as Gimbles, met their demise, Sears also was unable or unwilling to respond. The more than 500,000 employees and lumbering bureaucracy at Sears led one analyst to note that when compared with fleet-footed competition from K-Mart and Wal-Mart, Sears was a directionless 2,000-pound centipede with some of its 100 legs moving in different directions.

Hey, Buddy can you spare a minute?

On a recent visit to New York City, a university president was late for a meeting at the College Board. Leaving the Novotel Hotel, he hailed one of New York's numerous Yellow Cabs.

Having made the trip before, he knew it should take about ten minutes, which would get him there with at least a respectable lateness factor.

What the president didn't know was that the cab driver had no idea where the College Board office was located. After a 15-minute ride and a volatile argument over the meter charge, the president hit the pavement (not the driver) and hailed cab number two. Somewhat embarrassed he arrived at the meeting about 20 minutes past the appointed hour.

In an age of Quick Lube, microwaves, computerized hotel check-out, fax machines, and fast food, people have come to expect and demand speedy service.

One of the most memorable scenes of *Back to the Future* occurs when Michael J. Fox purchases a soft drink and attempts to twist off the top. That small indication of speed progress wasn't available a few years back. People had to stop and use the metal opener on the dispensing machine.

How many of us would go back to washing diapers or operator-assisted phone calls?

Not many.

Today we are a society of people who hate to be stuck in traffic, find out the item we want is out of stock, or have to wait more than a few minutes at a restaurant **unless** it is a fine dining establishment. Today we pump our own gas, bag our own groceries, and select our own shoes. We do so largely as a time-saving device. In addition, it saves us a few dollars.

What is our number one pet peeve? **Waiting in line**. A 1989 survey notes that over one-third of us can't stand waiting in long lines, particularly when other check-out stations are not open.

Pacesetters

With the prominence of speed becoming more and more important, are there any management efforts that should be mentioned?

Yes. Several.

Some of the pacesetting efforts have been founded on the pinstripe pronouncements of Yogi Berra, "You can observe a lot just by watching."

Reebok International founder, Paul Fireman, observed **permanency** in what other firms read as **fad**. There was a new need for sneakers beyond jogging. Many men and women wanted comfort and style and possibly more than one pair of sneakers. In only four years, 20 million customers discovered Reebok and sales jumped from $13 million to $1.4 billion.

Toys R Us quickly recognized the new working woman. They also realized, in contrast to Macy, that the old department store model was in for tough times. Today Toys R Us operates 250 stores with annual sales of more than $3 billion.

Some success in speed has been gained in small businesses.

Take mom-and-pop book stores. Although there are more than 3,000 major chain outlets for the big three book sellers, Barnes and Noble, B. Dalton, and Waldenbooks, 60% of the national sales occur at 6,000 privately owned book shops.

Why? Customers feel they get faster service from a knowledgeable staff.

The newly reorganized 7-Eleven chain is experimenting with the number one consumer complaint: long lines. With an already established image as a quick stop when compared to its supermarket competitors, many stores have two cashiers on duty at rush times.

A third approach to speed has been in terms of new products.

Witness the swiftness of the fast food business in response to the demand for fat-free or low-fat food.

McDonald's McLean Deluxe is probably the best known of these efforts. The 91% fat-free Carrageenan (Seaweed Extract) was introduced in April 1991. Kentucky Fried Chicken touted a new skinless creation, and Arby's also introduced a Lite Menu. In 1995, Taco Bell's "Border Lights" joined the low-fat parade. Burger King followed with Weight Watcher products.

- Four years ago there were approximately 600 low-fat or fat-free products on the market. Now there are almost 6,000.

- Many businesses have made speed breakthroughs by collapsing the time that elapses between design and delivery of a product.
- General Electric has compacted the manufacturing of circuit breaker boxes from three weeks to three days.
- Hewlett-Packard has short-sheeted its computer printer development from almost five years to slightly less than two.
- Brunswick has reduced its fishing reel time frame from three weeks to one.

Still other speed ups have come by utilizing technology and organizational modifications.

University Microfilms Inc. publishes doctoral dissertations at its Ann Arbor, Michigan headquarters. Growing steadily over the last decade, UMI built up a massive and growing backlog. In 1988 they had orders of 80,000 dissertations a year, but could only handle about one-fourth of that volume.

Taking stock of the situation, they soon learned that although it took 150 days for the company to process a thesis, less than one day was expended on a particular document. The other 149 days the dissertation sat on a shelf waiting for copyright approval, author response, or some other such item.

UMI has now reduced the processing time from 150 days to 2 months.

Bungee Jumpers

Bungee jumping is considerably new on the American scene. Billed as an activity that exceeds the excitement of a roller coaster ride and is somewhat akin to sky diving, a bungee jumper climbs aloft in a balloon and jumps free-fall style toward earth. These modern-day sky divers come complete with harness and umbilical cord. People who have tried it say that there is a tremendous "rush."

As the competition becomes more keen world wide, corporations large and small, government, education, and all other entities are going to have to crave such a rush.

Citicorp is now giving mortgage commitments in **15 minutes**.

Coke executives announced that they would do business with the Baltic Republics of Estonia, Latvia, and Lithuania long before the U.S.A. officially recognized the breakaway of the Soviet Republics.

Ford has recently authorized its dealers to spend up to $250 dollars to repair any unexpected customer problem.

In the fall of 1991 Arby's was the first fast food chain to accept credit cards at all of its 250 locations in 22 cities.

Kroger, at least in some of its stores, allows customers to check out their own groceries via electronic scanners.

Kellogg, a Battle Creek, Michigan breakfast cereal manufacturer, had boxes of Kellogg Frosted Flakes on market shelves featuring Tony the Tiger complete with Twins' pinstripes, monograph jersey and hat. They accomplished this feat **within 48 hours** after the final 1-0 Minnesota victory in the seventh game of the Series.

Fox TV announced only hours after Magic Johnson's AIDS Virus disclosure that it would be the first TV network to air condom ads.

Speed Kills
Much of the American mindset has come to be cautionary about speed.

Most of us are brought up to believe how great it is or would be to retain the Grover's Corner, New Hampshire atmosphere made famous by Thornton Wilder in *Our Town*. "Don't eat your food too fast," cautions your mother. "Don't be in such a hurry," concerned fathers say.

Perhaps it's time to re-examine the meaning of the road sign, "Speed Kills."

As we race for the year 2000, the culprit could well be **slowness**!

15

Downpowering

"What is needed is a management approach under which people will do what is right, develop and use new skills, focus on customer client relationships, and generally be involved in the business of which they are a vital part."

Joseph H. Boyette
Work Place 2000

When I was in graduate school, I shared an office with a colleague.

One day I walked into the office and asked him what he was doing. He said he was "decomposing." The strange look on my face must have signaled a lack of understanding on my part. He quickly added these words of clarification. "I wrote a long draft of this paper for class. Now I am going through it and making it shorter. I'm decomposing."

Looked at in this light, it is apparent that U.S.A. manufacturers have been decomposing for much of the past decade. Most, however, have been **downsizing without design.**

Corpocracy

During the past few years via mergers, cutbacks, retrenchments, layoffs, early retirements, and other adjustments, numerous manufacturers have downsized. DuPont eliminated 20% of its jobs, General Electric 25%. Among the Fortune 500 industrial companies, three and one-half millions jobs (more than 22%) were eliminated.

Between 1976 and 1988 IBM moved out 16,000 employees. By 1991 Big Blue had shed 55,000. In 1992 another 40,000 were farmed out.

McDonnell Douglas cut 17,000 workers in the 18 months between July 1990 and December 1991.

Burlington Northern Railroad has announced that 3,000 of its 8,500 brakemen are simply not needed anymore and plan on downsizing.

Caterpillar is divesting 10,000. GTE, 14,000. Tennaco has chopped off 8,000. Zenith is downsizing in a different manner. The Illinois based electronics firm plans to eliminate 1,000 jobs and move many of them to Mexico.

In late 1991 layoff announcements seemed to rival the speed of machine gun fire: Union Carbide, 5,500; First Interstate Bank, 3,350; Pacific Telesis, 3,000; Southwest Bell, 1,900; Frito-Lay, 1,800; American Express, 1,700; and the bullets wounded white and blue-collar workers alike. On one December day General Motors, TRW, and Xerox proclaimed they would trim 22,000 workers from the payrolls. Lotus Development Corporation said it would reduce its workforce by one in ten. As 1991 came to a close there were nearly **one million** unemployed professionals and mangers.

And while one management consulting firm, Arthur D. Little, calculated that six million white-collar jobs had been lost in the past six years, another firm, Morgan Stanley, noted that service payrolls were **still bloated** by nearly three million people.

Whittling

When I was a kid on my grandparents' Kentucky farm, I spent hundreds of hours observing my granddad's hobby: whittling. He would take a branch or a small piece of wood and start to carve. Sooner or later it would magically turn into something: a dog, a flower, a person. With great joy I would take the carving in hand and beam. "How do you know what it is going to be, Grandpa?" I would say. "I don't know," he would smile and say, "I just start whittling and the idea sort of comes to me."

A great many of our recent efforts at downsizing have come about in much that same manner.

Anyone can quickly see why the downsizing is necessary. American productivity has come to a crawl. Between 1958 and 1972 U.S.A. productivity averaged nearly 3%. Between 1973 and 1989, barely 1%.

And the problem was much worse in the large and growing service sector. Over the past decade blue-collar productivity has risen four times faster than the increase in white-collar production.

The fact is that much of the downpowering efforts have taken place in blue-collar industries. White-collar industries have only recently begun to get seriously involved. **Government** and **educational** institutions have yet to seriously approach reality.

While manufacturing firms were busily downsizing between July 1990 and June 1991, local and state government seemed oblivious and the federal government really didn't take downsizing seriously.

During this twelve-month period, government employment **went up** 200,000. State employment **grew** by 100,000. Federal employment was steady, but the rationale provides very little comfort. Two hundred thousand **temporary** Census workers were released.

College and university management doesn't have much to crow about either. From 1980 to 1990 higher education mid-level professionals **grew** by 62%.

Contrast the growth in local, state, and educational areas with the recent American Management Association survey. Of the 910 companies surveyed more than half had cut jobs between June 1990 and July 1991.

Large manufacturing firms seem to be well aware that downsizing is necessary. State government, local government, federal government, and education at all levels appear to be sitting by in ostrich-like fashion with their heads in a hole in the ground. The only trouble with that position is that it leaves one part of your anatomy in a very vulnerable position.

Downsizing

Downsizing means much more than frontline layoffs. It is a term directed at white-collar workers in any manufacturing or service industry, at mid-management, and top management. Although someone might argue that the practice will slacken as the national economy improves, downsizing will be a permanent change that affects the layers of management, the number of indirect workers, the span of empowerment, self-empowered work teams, and the frontline worker.

Delayering

David Johnson became Campbell Soup CEO in 1990. In 18 months he closed 20 plants and upped Campbell's plant utilization by 20%.

He also reduced headquarter staff by 300.

When Allied Signal, one of the nation's biggest conglomerates, announced that it would cut 5,000 jobs, the company also announced that most of the savings would come from eliminating layers of management in aerospace, engineering materials, and automotive products.

Ford in the early 80s wasn't doing particularly well. One of the major reasons was its overly generous management structure. When compared with Toyota with seven management layers, Ford had **twelve**.

When it comes to delayering the lesson can be clearly captured by looking at the actions of the 100 largest businesses in America. Since 1980 nine out of ten have reduced the **layers of management**.

Indirect Workers

In 1984 the Austin, Texas IBM circuit board factory was in big trouble. Several at headquarters thought the plant should be closed. But under the leadership of Jerry Carlson, Vice President and General Manager, a complete turn around was achieved.

In 1984 there were thre**e indirect** workers for every **direct** worker building circuit boards. Indirect tasks included repairing mistakes, maintaining machines, inspecting, and supervising. From a ratio of 3:1 circuit board production now reflects a 1:1 between direct and indirect workers.

Between 1950 and 1980, U.S.A.'s indirect (or nonproductive) workers increased five times as fast as those who actually did the producing. As Brunswick CEO, Jack Reichart, correctly summarizes, "We have been rewarding bookkeepers as if they created wealth. U.S. business has to make more beans rather than count them several times."

Span of Empowerment

One of the startling innovations to come out of this past decade is the clear understanding that American workers have been **over managed**. Part of this Taylor hangover is from the span of control necessitated by specific and fragmented jobs.

In the 1990s we will move away from the term "span of control" and shift toward terms like "span of empowerment" or "span of enablement."

Why? Competition and cost.

It stands to reason that with more people reporting to fewer supervisors that there would be substantial savings. One recent study is rather dramatic. One supervisor with three reporting workers costs **four times** as much as one supervisor with eight reporting workers.

The Frontline

One person who clearly understands the value of the frontline worker is the Dallas Cowboy running back, Emmitt Smith. Smith, who led the NFL in rushing during the 1991-92 and 1992-93 seasons, rewarded his linemen with Rolex watches in 1991-92 and a vacation of their choice in 1992-93.

Unfortunately, most American managers have not shown the same inclination toward the frontline.

As the 1989 MIT Commission on Industrial Productivity so aptly puts it, "There seems to be a systematic **undervaluation** of the frontline worker." Many managers still regard them as no more than cannon fodder.

American management's traditional regard for the frontline worker is best described by William Scott. Scott lumped all American workers into three broad categories: the significant small, the professional middle, and the insignificant mass. Sticking clearly with the old Taylor model, workers are to let executives think about goals, middle mangers concern themselves with results, and the frontline supervisor direct the methods. As a frontline worker you simply check your brain at the door.

American employers spend an excess of $30 billion each year on employee training. Only 8% of the money is spent on frontline workers. Most of that is a simple program of following Joe around. Few get any training after they are on the job. Most of the money is spent on top echelon training (without much bang for the buck)!

Enlightened American managers have come to understand that empowerment of the frontline is not only desirable, it is **absolutely necessary**. Only through involvement, understanding, responsibility, and an overall increase in the depth and breadth of the frontline will American productivity be able to improve.

Empowerment Teams

Although some firms like Procter & Gamble have been using empowerment groups or self-managed teams since the early 60s, this technique did not begin to catch on until the 1980s. At the close of the decade, 80% of the Fortune 1000 companies were attempting significant efforts at team empowerment, but few were using it at the frontline level.

Self-directed work teams are described by Jack Orsburn as groups of six to eighteen people who turn out a defined chunk of work, finished product, and/or service. The team concept is the exact opposite of Taylor's assembly line where each worker did only one small function.

Work teams are designed to have much more power and authority than the old Taylor worker. The intent is for the team to plan, organize, set goals, and to isolate and resolve problems.

Making Pancakes

The decade of the 90s is going to accentuate a flattening out in American management in every kind of enterprise: manufacturing, services, government, education, and all others. By the year 2000 the U.S.A. will speak in terms of management **pancakes** rather than management **pyramids**.

A Gallup Poll in early 1991 tells us why this **downpowering** must take place. Of the more than 1,200 organizations surveyed in terms of improving employee performance, the top suggestions were: letting employees put more ideas into action (33%), better management listening and supportive attitudes (30%), and employee skill training (20%).

The Glass Bottom

James R. Houghton is one chief executive officer that understands and exemplifies the downpowering movement in its true sense. Taking the reigns of the upstate New York Chemung River Valley Corning Company in 1983, he has breathed new life and **new culture** into the $3 billion corporation.

Houghton has **led** (not allowed) the downpowering.

In 1989 when Corning had to move its molten-metal fibers plant, the plant was turned over directly to teams of workers. Numerous job classifications were melded into one and the entire team worked in a close knit face-to-face manner. Workers were encouraged to rotate through jobs learning new skills and receiving higher pay.

What happened?

Defects were reduced so dramatically that the company went a full year with **zero** customer rejects.

In another instance a work team studied budget cutting and decided the actions to be taken. The plan saved Corning almost $500,000.

In September 1991 Paul O'Neill, the Chairman of Alcoa (Aluminum Company of America), began a determined effort at downpowering. Two levels of top management would be zapped while two dozen unit managers would be given maximum leeway.

Procter and Gamble's CEO John Smale has also been the proponent of significant downpowering. Procter and Gamble had 100 brand managers handling business that approached $1 billion annually. Time problems were typical where brand managers had to wait for three or four layers of management to make a decision. Promotional matters such as coupon sales would often have things like liquid and powdered soaps in the large company butting heads. Occasionally, even routine matters would be delayed up to a year.

The solution? Smale moved to **category management** with only 26 managers.

New products are now launched with a team made up of personnel from manufacturing, finance, and sales.

At one Campbell Soup plant in North Carolina, self-managed teams have virtually replaced supervisors. The teams establish their own scheduling. One new piece of capitol equipment selected by a self-managed team allowed for a double digit increase in productivity the first year.

Rightsizing

Demassing. Downsizing. Flattening. None of these terms really capture the need as well as **downpowering**. Downpowering must accompany the management goal of **rightsizing.** It is a calculated, goal-directed well studied effort, not a quick-draw shot in the dark. Goal one is to have fewer layers of management. Goal two must be to pass power to the frontline worker.

Downpowering is a term that you should get familiar with as soon as possible. Downpowering is not a fad. A robust economy will not erase the need to do it. Downpowering is avoiding creeping bureaucracy. Those close to the action — customers and markets — need the O. K. to make decisions.

You are going to have to downpower in **your** organization!

16

Great Expectations

"The optimist invented the airplane, the pessimist the parachute."

Anonymous

Jump and Shoot

It is an accepted practice for after-dinner speakers to first tell a joke or an amusing anecdote before getting into the meat of the speech. The reasoning is that it gives the audience a chance to relax and ease into the material which is yet to come.

Imagine the round table, stained white linen, silverware, and dirty dishes as you learn the lesson of expectations as told in the story of the hunter and the panther.

An accomplished marksman was hunting for the only trophy that had ever eluded him. Having been on the hunt for quite some time, he was returning to his campsite when he heard sounds in the nearby brush.

He approached cautiously and saw the illusive black panther he sought. As he leveled his rifle to fire the animal saw him. Just as he fired the gun the panther jumped over him and ran off.

Dismayed, the hunter returned to his campsite and practiced his shooting.

The next morning he returned to the area where he had last seen the panther. Again he heard noise in the brush. He carefully moved the bushes aside. The hunter didn't expect what he saw. The panther was practicing **his** jumps!

The hunter didn't expect what he saw and you didn't expect "jumps" to be the punch line (unless you already heard the story). Things don't always work out as expected.

Imagine how surprised Florida Power and Light was after developing super surge protectors for power lines, only to find out that the power outages that had plagued them were caused by vultures excreting on their insulators.

Expectations are paralyzing notions when they can't be met. Consider the case of lines and lemons.

Lines and Lemons

If you have ever gone rushing into the grocery store on the way home from work to pick up "just a few items" or tried to cash a check during your lunch hour, you know first-hand the agony of standing in line.

Unless you're a Type A personality undergoing therapy or Type B and don't care, the experience can be frustrating. Being 10 customers away from "may I help you" (assuming you ever hear those words) with no time to waste is a perplexing experience. The defense that checkers and tellers need a break too isn't satisfactory.

Convenience stores and ATMs are two niche markets borne from the problem of standing in line. People have less time to conduct their business so they expect 1st class service at the bulk rate.

If it isn't a line it's a lemon. In the case of automobiles the adage, "if someone gives you a lemon, make lemonade" is impractical advice. Many consumers have had the misfortune of driving a shiny new vehicle off the dealer lot only to find that it doesn't work the way it should. It wasn't long ago that the best U.S. automobiles were equivalent to the worst of those being built abroad.

Recent attention to quality and customer satisfaction have turned the "lemon" tide for the moment. There has been a strong, general advance in the quality of American cars in the last few years. Defects in American cars are now on par with the European automakers but still twice as many per vehicle as Japan.

This is not enough, however, in an industry where customer loyalty can generate $150,000 over one person's lifetime of car buying. Customers expect better.

Consumer fraud has become big business. Attorney General's offices in many states have created specialty divisions to handle it. "Lemons" apparently are recession proof. The make-it-right-the-first-time tactics of American enterprise still need improvement.

Lines and lemons make a statement to the consumer. It is a statement about inefficiency, neglect, and blind faith. When American business does not offer quality products or services and consumers are willing to accept "made in the U.S.A." because it's their only alternative, something has to change.

It did. The globe got smaller, government regulation changed, and higher quality foreign products found their way into American pocket books. American business woke up with a migraine headache.

Maybe consumers **expected too much**?

Sir James Jeans, a British astronomer and author, was asked to explain the long, happy life he enjoyed with his wife. Jeans said, "blessed are they who expect nothing for they shall not be disappointed."

Jeans' explanation might be enough to explain past consumer attitudes. The days of lowered expectations which caused consumers to be very happy over very little are gone. Consumers have learned to expect a lot from the products and services they buy and those who provide them.

Many references are made to "Pandora's Box." To set the record straight, it was Pandora's servant who really opened the box. Pandora immediately rushed to close it before any creature could escape. Unfortunately, one creature did get out. It was **hope**.

The buying public has not lost hope. In fact, their hope has been renewed. Today's successful businesses are characterized by the ability to deliver on the lofty expectations of customers. Today's definition of expectation is quality, choice and service.

Innocent but Incarcerated

It is easy to remember when almost everyone used a rotary-dial phone. It didn't seem particularly inconvenient at the time. The best feature of using a rotary-dial phone was that the caller connected with the person they wanted to reach. Seven little turns of the dial, a few rings, and the caller's expectations were met. The conversation could begin.

Rotary-dial was replaced by touchtone dialing. Everyone seemed pleased by the progress. Unfortunately, those happy little touchtone sounds led to yet another technological advance. Welcome to voice-mail! It didn't take long for the journey to go from *voice-mail* to *voice-*

jail. In the process, the road to improved customer service made a U-turn.

Suddenly, innocent people trying to buy goods or services or to complain about them were welcomed into this labyrinth of technology by a "friendly" voice and the words "Press one...now." After numerous pre-recorded messages and voice-traps like *pound* and *asterisk* the innocent quickly land in voice-jail: a never-never land of micro-chips, fiber optic cable, and digitized voice.

The number of confused, exasperated, and angry cutomers lost to this technological maze is unknown.

Voice-mail has reduced customer service to a sophisticated, high-tech numbers game.

Its alter ego, "voice-mail-jail," is the unjustified and unnecessary incarceration of the innocent.

The 44% Solution

It wasn't really too many years ago that choice was no choice at all. The Bavarian immigrant Levi Strauss sold canvas pants to gold miners in California. Today, his namesake company offers styles for men, women, and children in many different varieties. Henry Ford wanted to build a black car for everyone. Today, shopping for a car can be a career. There are more than 600 makes and models to choose from.

If consumers don't want the shopping mall hassle, they can pick between the Home Shopping Network (HSN) or Quality Value Club (QVC) and shop by television.

Try to select a variety of Campbell's soup. It can be M'm! M'm! TOUGH! There are 70 different choices.

Ice cream has come a long way from plain vanilla. In consuming approximately 1.4 billion gallons of ice cream last year, choosy consumers picked from varieties as different as Rocky Road, Bubblegum, and Pina Colada. There is beer flavored ice cream too. And yogurt has complicated the choice parade.

In communication, we can pick from voice, data, text, or image. Searching for long distance service? Try AT&T, MCI, or SPRINT. Sneakers are available in over 1,000 styles. Toothpaste provides over 100 different choices.

After deciding what to eat, choice requires a selection of salt, low salt, no salt, or salt substitute. Remember to spread margarine or butter on the dinner roll. If they won't eat what their parents eat, kids can choose from Circus O's, Spaghetti O's, Sporty O's, or Teddy O's. If they are still unsure, "Let Mikey try it!"

Choice has become an obsession.

Consumers want choice and they have it. The complication for business is to try and understand what Donald Petersen calls **customer's reality**.

Understanding the reality takes a correct mixture of persistence and smarts. One way to do it is by getting close and staying close to the customer. It's similar to what Mark Twain said about cats. A person who grabs a cat by the tail knows 44% more about cats than those who don't.

This is the 44% solution of customer satisfaction.

Action Speaks Louder than Words

It is time to reshape and refocus management attitudes toward the customer. Customers must be the core value of the organization. Place a value on one satisfied customer. Then consider that satisfied customers will always tell others about their experiences. So will those who are dissatisfied. The vast majority of a company's dissatisfied customers never complain they just end their relationship with the company (and its products or services).

Solectron, a California manufacturing company that won a Baldrige Award makes sure this doesn't happen to them. They call each of their customers to see if they got the products on time and are satisfied.

"Have it your way" is the Burger King marketing slogan used to help distinguish it from the competition in the crowded but very lucrative fast food business.

Burger King's CEO asked the company's employees to make "have it your way" more than just hamburger preparation. He wanted the slogan to become the mindset for how Burger King operates. The message was received.

When a customer called company representatives after dining in a Burger King where a light was out, a computer was used to notify the restaurant's manager. With the light quickly fixed, the manager drove across town, picked up the couple, brought them back to the restaurant and served up free Whoppers and fries.

These very satisfied customers had it their way!

Southwest Airlines became the industry leader with a low fare, short-haul, emphasis on customer formula. Other airlines have tried to mimic the formula but Southwest Airlines just keeps winning. As Continental and United tried to "catch" Southwest, the airline accelerated its expansion — adding 29% more routes in 1994.

Those with a short-term view miss the point. The cost of creating new customers is much higher than keeping old ones. Fashion specialty retailer Nordstrom has adopted a corporate culture that understands this principle.

Customer satisfaction is something they **do**, not something they **talk** about. Psychologists suggest that talking about things is the way people avoid doing them. The only rule a Nordstrom sales person has to learn is to use their best judgement in doing whatever it takes to make the customer happy.

Refunds are accepted or exchanges made without question. Sales personnel (notice that they are not called clerks) are given a wide range of authority and responsibility to respond to customer wants. The corporate pyramid is literally turned upside down to reflect the attitude that their managers are there to support frontline workers. Nordstrom's sales revenue of $2.8 billion in 1990 points out the bottom-line value of customer service, in terms of customer expectation.

To retain current customers and gain new ones, organizations must be wiser, quicker, tougher, better, and more consistent in meeting their expectations. It's a lot like the team that wins the Super Bowl. It is difficult to stay on top. It takes both hard work and smart work to maintain excellence.

An optional driver's side air bag was installed by the Saturn Corporation two years ahead of schedule. In response to dealers who said they were losing buyers, Saturn accelerated its schedule to meet customer expectations.

The consumer product giant Proctor and Gamble knows that consumers have changed their attitudes about health and fitness. They are looking for more nutritious food products. One was found. The company is only FDA approval away from **zero fat**. It's called Olestra.

Not everyone's on the customer service turnstile. On April 25, 1995 the First Chicago Bank announced it will charge customers for visiting a **live** teller if they could have used an ATM machine. "Thanks for your business, that will be $3.00 please!"

TWA gave new meaning to "comfort zone" when it announced that it would remove between 10 and 40 seats from each of its 166 jets to create more leg room for passengers. There is some financial risk for the financially plagued carrier, but the emphasis on choice flight accommodations for consumers represents a return to the high quality service for which TWA was once known.

Marriott's division of hotels, resorts, and suites is undergoing an expectation transformation by implementing Total Quality Management (TQM). Simply stated, TQM is the application of quality standards to everything the company does, including satisfying its customers.

By 1992 all 100,000 employees in the division were trained in TQM. Like Nordstrom, hourly employees as well as management are empowered to do whatever it takes to please the customer.

Marriott management understands that customers have become much more sophisticated. They want the customer to find that at Marriott.

Marriott's customer response system is their way of grabbing the cat by the tail.

The "cat" knows all about check-in, reservations, room cleanliness, wake-up calls, friendliness of staff, and how the morning coffee tastes. Travelers who are curious about what happens to those "how are we doing" questionnaires after they are completed might like to know what happens next.

At Marriott customer responses are quantified into a Guest Services Index for each hotel. The company's employee bonus structure is then tied to the index. Some customer responses have even elicited a personal letter from the company CEO, Bill Marriott, Jr. In other words, they are used to keep Marriott on top of the hospitality industry. The customer response surveys done by *Business Travel News* bear out Marriott's superstar status.

Not every company winning the expectations game is a seasoned veteran. Some are rookies. Take Gateway 2000. They have shown a five year compounded growth rate of 26,500%. This level of growth was achieved after just 5 years in business. Gateway 2000 is in the personal computer business and competition is both exhilarating and brutal. Despite the obstacles, Gateway 2000 has done very well. They are one of a number of companies that took a huge chunk of IBM's market. A market where shipments of IBM PCs dropped from 61% to 18% during a six year period.

The company's 33 year old founder has a theory about why. It has to do with the customer and value. His view is that PCs either have too many technological gadgets and gizmos to be affordably priced or they are skeleton units that are basically useless. Neither offers the customer any real value.

Gateway 2000 is a mail order PC business that successfully found the middle ground. Technology is added only when it offers the customer **real value**. The company is apparently on the right track, with $275 million in 1990 sales and a number one ranking in the 1991 *Inc.*

Gateway 2000 avoided being a casualty of the belief that you can be on the right track and still get run over.

Great Expectations? A good novel, but if you don't meet their expectations in the 1990's your customers are going to give you the dickens!

17

PSSST!

"Successful organizations are transforming the structures that bind them."

Dan Angel

SOS

●●● - - - ●●●. Three dots, three dashes, and three more dots. When sounded, the combination signals an SOS. These symbols, adopted from the Morse telegraphic alphabet, are universally known distress signals. They are commonly used by ships to communicate trouble. The dot-dash sequence was picked because it has a distinctive sound and is easy to transmit.

The exact meaning of the acronym SOS is not known. Because of its relationship to sea travel, Save Our Ship is the most agreed upon translation. It has also been translated to mean Save Our Soul and Sure Of Sinking. SOS became the name for a not-so-popular army breakfast. It even found its way into employment.

A group of job applicants were sitting in the lobby of a company, each waiting to be interviewed for one available job. Over the loud speaker a Morse Code signal was quietly sounded. The signal stated that any applicant who understood the message should get up and go into the interviewer's office. Upon doing so, the only person to **understand** the message was offered the job.

This would certainly be an unusual basis for a contemporary hiring decision but, as the story goes, the boss wanted to hire the most attentive person available. The idea is valid. **Attention** is an important attribute. Attention is being **aware** and, more importantly, being **receptive** to what is going on. Management attention to a changing work environment and what the changes mean about structure, process, people and thinking might help organizations avoid sending out their own SOS.

Organizations have never intentionally planned for the day when they will have to send out an SOS. To the contrary, they plan for high performance and results. Despite good intentions and careful planning, business, education, and government are all sounding SOS in alarming numbers.

Many corporate executives, elected officials, and educational leaders are searching for the correct combination to make organizations operate effectively and efficiently. Certainly stockholders and stakeholders want them to succeed.

Some organizations **do** succeed. They are able to arrange the parts in symmetry with understood and accepted goals and achieve a new level of success. Others get lucky and succeed in spite of themselves. However, the vast majority are looking for Waldo.

Therein lies the problem. There are no permanent answers. There is no single solution. Organizations seeking success today have to be flexible and dynamic. Success isn't found on a one way street.

Transformational Thinking

One interpretation of SOS that has yet to be offered describes the straight jacket that American organizations have slipped into. Think of SOS as the **stricture of structure**. For nearly all of the 20th century structure has been synonymous with control, restraint, limits, and predictability. Structure has been designed to control people and actions. Successful organizations are transforming the structures that bind them.

The past is not really gone. The November 25, 1991 *Business Week* cover shows 5 CEOs under the caption "Tough Times, Tough Bosses." The feature story describes CEOs comfortable with slice and cut, slash and burn tactics.

What is needed is **transformational thinking**, not tough bosses. That song has been played before. Transformational thinking means that the captains of industry and other organizational chieftains cultivate new skills and managerial style. Transformation means tossing many traditional organizational practices out the window.

In Copenhagen, Denmark the Oticon Company has done just that. Oticon is the third largest manufacturer of hearing aids in the world. Manufacturing a product for only the one person in twenty who needs one is not easy. The company's risk of operating against the norm is substantial.

If you were to walk through the company's office (yes, only one) you might be amazed to see the "President" sitting in an open office area with the clerks, designers, and engineers. Everyone literally works together. The company has even removed the elevators to encourage meetings among employees. No one at Oticon has a permanent desk. Letters don't even leave the mail room.

In an effort to reduce the flow of paper by 80% all necessary incoming mail is computer scanned in the mail room and the junk mail discarded. If employees get tired of their current job it is not a long-term problem. Every employee can bid on each job that comes along and job rotation is a part of how the company operates.

Converting from the traditional organizational arrangement to the **open workplace** is not without costs. The reforms at Oticon are expected to result in losses, or at best, break even for a couple of years. One of the expected benefits of integrating their workforce is that eventually products will be brought to production in half the current time.

Are the costs worth it? Everyone at Oticon thinks so. Their belief is that changing the way the company operates is the only way to be competitive in the next century. They are willing to assume short-term losses for **long-term gain**.

The age of information has changed the way organizations function. Competition has never been as fierce. Technology has changed both the rules and the operating environment. Organizations are being flattened. Middle management is becoming the modern day dino-saur and moving toward extinction.

Customer service, innovation, speed, quality, and teamwork are the suggested virtues of the new corporate culture. Corporations have embarked on **concept-to-customer thinking**. A sort of alpha-omega path. Many are attempting to negotiate this high risk path.

What is learned along the path is to arrange organizations around the production capabilities of mass, the craft standards of quality, and the lean potential of people. A promising solution might be found by *promoting structures, skills, strategies, and thinking* (PSSST) that work.

Kaleidoscope

Organizational structures haven't changed much during the 20th century. Choose any industry. Pick from autos, food, health care, apparel, textiles or steel. Add financial services, consumer electronics, commercial aircraft, or chemicals and pharmaceuticals to the deck. Pick a card. Any card.

In most industries, the primary relationships among people in the workplace are still largely vertical. Vertical relationships are fostered by clearly defined hierarchies. Individuals and jobs serve as the foundation of hierarchies. Skills, teams, flexibility, and cooperation are untapped attributes.

Things are changing. Organizations are reducing layers, creating autonomous units, fostering innovation, encouraging worker flexibility, and developing internal and external partnerships.

Consider one better idea.

At Ford the first Taurus rolled off the assembly line in 1986. Taurus was described as a driver's car. It got the description because those who designed it were told to produce a car that **they** would like to drive. The Taurus achieved outstanding results. The achievements occurred as a result of how it was produced.

The traditional way of building a car was exchanged for a bold new approach to produce the Taurus. It brought together operationally three concepts that Ford's CEO Donald Peterson held dear. **Participative management, employee involvement**, and **teamwork programs** were the heart and soul of the Taurus development.

The idea was to integrate designers, product engineers, manufacturing engineers, and marketing specialists from the beginning of the project and give them the freedom to do what they do best. The result was a car that customers wanted to drive and a spirit inside the company which caused employee revitalization.

The Team Taurus project taught Ford a valuable lesson. It has changed the way Ford does business. The team approach now involves suppliers as well so that expectations are clear in advance and they too can join in the company's commitment to excellence. Ford is not the only company to achieve results through teamwork.

3M built an alpha-omega path by combining design, production, and marketing units into one cohesive unit. The reason? They learned from a previous effort that **teams** produce results.

3M's digital color proofer was developed by a team approach that cut development time from 6 to 3 years. The commercial printing industry which was the target market benefitted most from the improved cycle time. *Consumers are time starved.*

Corning, Inc. has also employed the team approach successfully. Quality is the goal that unites the thousands of teams created by Corning. Their purpose is to achieve **total customer satisfaction**. Bringing disparate units together has produced big results for the company. The company's major divisions of consumer products, laboratory services, special materials, and communications are all better able to serve their customers by utilizing the internal network strategy.

Corning has extended the philosophy to their relationship with their Glass Blowers Union. Worker teams determine job skills and even factory design. In the near future all Corning U.S. workers will share in a bonus based on plant performance.

It isn't easy to develop **horizontal linkages**. Yet experience has shown that organizations can become too large. They are like freighters trying to turn. Just about the time the turning is complete, the wind changes direction. One way to turn faster is to put some of your products on a separate ship. IBM has recently adopted this approach.

IBM announced two downsizing ventures that reduced the payroll by 40,000 employees. It wasn't enough. The computer giant also announced plans to spin-off two divisions into separate operating units and give greater autonomy to another.

The Pennant Systems Company plans to develop and manufacture advanced printers and related software. The Storage Products Company will handle the disk drive business. The personal computer division will have much greater authority in decision making. The decision making hierarchy will be reduced from 30 to 10. With this new autonomy in hand, place a bet on IBM joining the mail order computer business. Despite the company's significant overhead costs, the competition may leave them no choice.

Even with these changes, CEO John Akers couldn't avoid the axe. Early 1993 brought announcement of the largest annual loss in history, a stock dividend cut, and the departure of three senior IBM officials.

The idea for companies like IBM is to build **independence** and **accountability** into each business unit and respond to the challenge posed by smaller, more agile manufacturers. Gateway 2000, Dell, and Compaq computers have helped remodel the computer industry and forced companies like IBM to adapt to a higher risk, change oriented operating environment.

Like IBM, Emerson Electric also made similar changes when it combined like technology divisions into business groups. The goal was to sell related products from different groups together for the company's largest customers.

Transformational thinking isn't reserved for corporations. When the Rochester, New York school system embarked on dramatic change, it started out with a partnership between old adversaries. The superintendent and the head of the union brought people together to determine what students should know and how this knowledge would be measured. They also were the first school system to implement **site-based management**. SBM is a way to push decision making down to the local level. It is being widely adopted by other school systems.

Vertical is out. Horizontal is in. But there are times and places for each. One will never completely replace the other. Organizational designs need to evolve like the shapes in a kaleidoscope. The designs in a kaleidoscope are variegated and changing but always orderly. All the pieces fit together. It is one lesson worth learning. There are others.

School Days

If there is a corporate malaise then some of the blame has to be shared by education and by everyone else who let us become non-competitive. America's education system is in the same global marketplace as business and government. It must be capable of at least meeting the world's standards. For America to dominate it must **exceed** them.

In America's inner cities the wasted human potential is a national disgrace. Imagine schools where a history teacher has 110 students and 26 books or the chemistry teacher who uses a popcorn popper as a Bunsen burner. Think about the school where water cascades down the stairways when it rains. These examples are not the product of a wild imagination. They are reality in East St. Louis, Chicago, and South Bronx. Shame won't help America win the education race.

Corporate America depends on the educational system. Too many businesses are being asked to spend millions teaching what the schools did not teach. $30 billion is spent annually by corporations on workplace training.

Also, much time is spent debating whether the schools have failed the nation or the nation has failed the schools. The hour is late. What matters is resolving the problem. Both the friends and critics of education need to remember the saying, "schools are four walls with tomorrow inside."

Many experts suggest that Japan's success in the global marketplace is traced to the efficiency of its schools. American's efficiency needs to reach a similar level in every school in every town.

The solutions are not complicated. The National Center on Education and the Economy published a report on the skills of the American workforce. The report, *America's Choice: High Skills or Low Wages* calls for revolutionary changes.

The report urges:
- A new national educational performance standard that is benchmarked to the world's highest.
- States to ensure that all students achieve a certificate of initial mastery by age 16.
- A comprehensive system of training for students not seeking a baccalaureate degree.
- Incentives to encourage employees to invest in further education and training for workers.
- Employment training boards to oversee school to work transition programs and training systems.

Excuses won't do. Some have said America may have the worst school to work transition of any advanced industrial country. There is **no way** to excuse that!

America 2000, a public policy strategy, describes the necessary goals for improving the nation's educational system. By the year 2000, the strategy suggests that American school children should (1) start school ready to learn, (2) leave 4th, 8th, and 12th grade competent in English, Math, and History, and (3) be first in the world in Math & Science.

The strategy also calls for increasing the graduation rate to 90% (currently 83%), ensuring adult literacy, and decreasing drug use and violence in schools.

When 1,000 adults were asked to compare U.S. public education with that of Japan, Great Britain, and Germany, 53% described it as **weak**. If the U.S. is to remain competitive into the next century **anemic** won't cut it.

It doesn't matter what the structure is if those who occupy it aren't skilled enough to do the work. The best description of the current circumstance is that American workers are over-managed and under educated. As a result, we need more schooling and less tooling.

Bubbles

Kids who participate in scouting are taught to use a compass. This simple device helps scouts determine which direction to go. Although the compass only points in one direction it provides the relative direction of any other pole. In other words, locating one direction can lead you in many directions. The organizational compass is called strategy. People who develop strategy should be mindful of the most important admonition of the compass. *A compass can be fooled.* What causes it to work can also cause its undoing.

Strategies are both good and bad, effective and ineffective. Some strategies are casual and shortsighted. Others are skillful. Some strategies are crafted carefully while others are haphazard.

American Express thought it had a winning strategy to market a prestige credit card. The company targeted only the high-end market, the elite clientele. In reacting to the competition from other card issuers they broadened their strategy and became more inclusive. American Express wasn't widely accepted by the masses and their original target market started leaving home without them.

Phillip Morris has not been successful in shedding its tobacco-only image. Despite strategic acquisitions such as General Foods and Miller Brewing it still isn't regarded as a consumer-products company. Kraft General Foods is the newest attempt at creating a diversified strategy.

Few people have heard of a bubble strategy. That's what CBS used when it entered into the four-year, $1 billion contract with Major League Baseball. The original strategy was deceptively sound but soon burst into nothing. CBS lost $500 million.

Frito-Lay has a simple strategy that works. Get close to the customer and stay there. Mix this closeness with an emphasis on taste. Frito-Lay's strategy has led them to be called the Mozart of the snack food industry.

The Aprex Corporation has developed the "smart" bottlecap that is equipped with its own chip, alarm clock, and tiny display. It counts the number of times the bottle is opened each day. If the patient isn't following the doctor's orders, "dosing partners" will call the next day to remind them.

Toys R Us went global in 1984. After years of trying, the company recently opened its first Japanese store. Toys R Us appears to have implemented a successful strategy to break into the Japanese toy market. TRU plans to open 10 new stores per year in Japan through the end of the decade. Japan is a $6 billion market. It's too early to tell if the strategy will pay off but successful history is on their side.

Wal-Mart Stores, Inc. is going to go head-to-head with national brands in the product market. It has introduced Sam's Choice Cola in red and white cans that look vaguely familiar to those sold by the world's number one selling cola.

The Lesson

The whole idea is to create a structure that works, fill it with skilled people, give them the freedom to use strategic resources and let them attend to helping the organization achieve maximum results! PSSST!

When management adapts to *promoting structure, skill, strategy, and thinking* that work, SOS will signal the **Spirit Of Success**.

18

Warriors

"The markets are going to get intensely more competetive than they are today."

George Fisher
Chairman and CEO
Motorola, Inc.

That was Then

What were you doing the year that "streaking" became a fad? That same year "The Sting" was awarded Best Picture and Jack Lemmon and Glenda Jackson won Oscars for Best Actor and Actress. Johnny Miller established a single season earnings record for golfers by pocketing $346,000 and Woodward and Bernstein published "All the President's Men." Ali was still fighting (and winning), Patricia Hearst joined the Symbionese Liberation Army, and Little League Baseball, Inc. voted to allow girls to play. These events seem like they happened only yesterday.

Imagine! Events we experienced first-hand can only be viewed historically by students entering college for the first time. Time passes quickly whether you're having a good time or not.

The year was 1974

In 1974, there was worldwide inflation, most industrialized nations had zero economic growth, and in the United States wage and price controls were finally lifted. In 1974, Japan was just a country soundly defeated by the United States in a previous conflict or the imprint on the bottom of vacation souvenirs. Europe was a hodge-podge of friend and foe.

Today, we live in a world that is changing so fast that most of us find it difficult to keep up. Twenty years ago, people lived in a town or a city. No one claimed residency beyond a country. Today we all live in a world.

This is Now

We live in a world that has changed a lot. Those who believe that the United States is still all that matters need to be reminded of some important facts. The U.S. has only 5% of the world's 5 billion population and accounts for just 25% of the world's industrial productivity.

The U.S. tradition of strength in the world's economy is being eroded by big muscle: Japan, Germany, and other Pacific Rim countries like Taiwan and Korea.

A study by the Office of Technology Assessment shows that the U.S. has lost a share of the world manufacturing market and the standard of living has fallen to 1960s levels for many American workers engaged in manufacturing.

The Council on Competitiveness asked 1,000 Americans if America's ability to compete is declining. Three out of four respondents said, "Yes." Asked whether Japan was ahead of the United States in economic competitiveness, 77% of those answering also said, "Yes."

Three towers of American strength are now owned by Japanese interests. Rockefeller Center, the Time and Life Building, and the McGraw-Hill building in New York belong to the Mitsubishi Estate Company. It doesn't matter that the properties were a bad investment. More important, they leave an impression of **competitive weakness**.

Names like Sony, Hitachi, Nissan, and Toshiba are as common to American consumers as Chevrolet, Magnavox, Pillsbury, and Holiday Inn. European imports, such as Germany's BMW, Sweden's Volvo, and Italy's Porsche, are as well known in the United States as any homegrown model.

The first fiber optic cable across the Atlantic ocean went into service in 1988. In 1989 another went into service across the Pacific. The linkages between east and west and the Pacific Rim have been growing stronger and stronger.

The World According to Garp was a good name for a Hollywood movie. Today's world can be described according to another G word. It isn't Garp. The new G stands for **global**. A global economy, global competition, global wealth, global technology, global communication, and global transportation help make up the global factor. Examples of the global factor are everywhere.

- Delta's 600 million dollar acquisition of Pan American routes landed the airline in 21 international cities and its European hub in Frankfurt, Germany.
- Taiwan aerospace bought 40% of McDonnell Douglas's commercial airline business for $2 million amidst concerns of transferring more American technology abroad.
- Japan's largest pharmaceutical company features Arnold Schwarzenegger to promote the company's vitamin fortified drink.
- *Newsweek* publishes a Korean language edition in a joint

venture with a Korean newspaper.

- Fifty thousand Moscowvites a day sample hamburgers at an icon of western culture: McDonald's.
- Halliburton was the first American engineering and construction company to oversee the planning, design, and construction of a Japanese real estate property.
- Britain's Marks and Spencer, one of the world's best retailers, has purchased Brooks Brothers 53 U.S. stores.
- 80% of Coca-Cola's operating profit comes from overseas.
- Mickey, Minnie, Goofy, and Pluto have new residences in France and Japan.
- A Japanese version of Mattel's Barbie failed miserably. Reintroduced in Japan exactly as they are sold in America (blonde hair and all) the doll became a big seller.

It's getting hard to know if we are **them** or they are **us**. Either way, ideas, technology, products and services are just part of the international parade. As a result the **rules of competition** will never be the same again.

Bye, Bye, American Pie

Winston Churchill once observed that empires of the future will be empires of the mind. His comments are an important harbinger for American business, education, and government. If you want to be a leader in today's global marketplace you have to be smart. In other words, what you don't know can't help you.

The spread of **knowledge** and **information** throughout the world has changed the rules of competition at home and abroad. Knowledge has been described as the explosive force behind the tough competitive environment organizations are forced to operate in today.

The spread of knowledge and its application to new products has caused American firms to spend record amounts on Research and Development. While leading in dollars spent on R&D America is behind the global competition in exploiting it for commercial purposes. Sixty-seven cents out of each research dollar is spent on defense. Spinoffs from research in the defense industry eventually make their way to the commercial markets. The problem is that they result more from **coincidence** than **direct** effort.

There are companies converting research dollars into commercial success. Consider the R&D efforts of the number one Microelectronics and Computer Consortium (MCC) in the U.S. The consortium has been granted 64 patents since 1987. The most recent development will allow volume production of world class semiconductors.

Pfizer, a U.S. pharmaceutical company, has enjoyed many victories in the global marketplace. The firm has spent $3.5 billion on new product development. Even when the company's profit margins suggested a conservative course, Pfizer emphasized research productivity.

Companies outside the U.S. are searching worldwide for R&D opportunities which support their product development. Often they find it in the United States. Nova Industry of Denmark invests heavily in U.S. biotechnology research to support their enzyme and insulin products.

In the new global environment **ideas** travel **fast**. They become multinational as fast as the organizations that produce them. They are adapted and improved and return as someone else's idea.

Consider what American innovation in technology has done to products around the world. Technology developed in the U.S. re-emerges elsewhere in a new, cheaper, and often improved form. A number of well known commodities have been born of American ingenuity only to be transferred elsewhere. The list includes automobiles, steel, television, and recently, commercial aircraft. Products such as oxygen furnaces, microwave ovens, and videocassette recorders, should also be counted.

This is how it works. The technology is sold directly or comes wrapped as part of a sell-off of company assets used to improve cash flow, reduce profit pressures, or change the perception of Wall Street analysts. The technology is quickly transformed by cheap labor, lower production costs, higher quality, and/or better distribution.

In some cases nationalism helps speed the transformation. Governments provide financial support to encourage product development. It has been a classic strategy of the Japanese to pair industry and government in partnership to bring an emerging technology to the commercial market. Governments in Europe bankroll the airbus industry, an industry that represents 28% of the commercial airplane manufacturing business in the world.

In the U.S. corporations often invest heavily in the business of government but not vice versa. The large defense contractor, Northrop, has 50% of its total revenues tied to production of the B-2 Stealth Bomber. Northrop's revenues depend on decisions of the U.S. Congress. If the government stops production they must quickly change direction or suffer harsh financial consequences.

Japan, Inc.

In the early 1980s Japan excelled in three areas of new ideas and new products. Most of Japan's innovations were found in instruments to measure time, internal combustion engines, and photography. Their research and development emphasis was directed primarily at these three areas.

By 1991 Japan had surged ahead in 10 times as many technologies. Thirty different technologies including photocopying, magnetic information storage and retrieval, radiation chemistry, office machines, image analysis, solid state electronics and television are just some of Japan's leading-edge accomplishments today.

Innovations in Japan are no accident. They are the result of consistent focus in two areas. First, they are spending substantial amounts on R&D and, second, their R&D expenditures are planned under government direction to reduce unnecessary duplication.

Patent activity offers a clue to U.S. innovation woes. The 35 classes of technology in which Japanese companies were most interested include 11 that were of least interest to U.S. firms. These include information storage and retrieval, photography, photocopying, printing and office machinery, and motor vehicles.

On the other hand, of the 35 technologies of highest activity in U.S. firms, only 4 were of interest to Japanese companies. They were tobacco, ammunition and explosives, universal oil processes and products, and wells.

There is something wrong with this picture!

Whether the technology is transformed in partnership with government or not, the result is the same. Once developed it behaves like a **boomerang**. The technology returns as a new product to create competitive advantage for its producer organization.

In some cases, even a simple idea can become someone else's gold mine.

Turtles and Trucks

If the patent activity between the early 80s and early 90s is a good measure of this advantage, then the U.S. is on the wrong side of the success curve. Take the case of Rafael, Donatello, Leonardo, and Michelangelo. These are the four reptiles known to millions as the

Teenage Mutant Ninja Turtles. Rejected by two U.S. firms as too big a financial risk, they were picked up by Hong Kong based Playmates.

Originated as a comic strip by two American cartoonists, the Turtles have made Playmates the most profitable toy company in history.

It wouldn't be at all surprising to learn that the machines used to make all those Turtles come from America. Even American machines are in global hands.

Corporate executives who are busy fighting the international competition are often reminded that there is still competition at home.

Take the case of Cummins Engines. They challenged the Japanese in the heavy-duty truck engine market and won. Winning turned into losing when their domestic rival Detroit Diesel took advantage of their distraction and made a substantial dent in Cummins market share.

Dough Wars

The battleground of competition is fierce in the 15 billion dollar pizza industry. The main rivals include Pizza Hut, the nation's largest, Domino's, Little Caesar, and Pizza Inn.

The most important ingredient in these dough wars isn't dough. It is home delivery. Thirty minutes is the industry standard. Domino's offers a $3 discount if the pizza arrives late. They even have one outlet that delivers by boat. Casino's Pizza outlets took Domino's offer up a notch. If it's not there in 30 minutes, the pizza is free.

Other pizza firms have tried new approaches to seize their share of the pizza prize. Casa Luna, a Chicago firm, offers video rentals in its pizza shops to attract customers. Shakey's is diversifying its menu into pasta and tacos in order to achieve market advantage.

Not far from the main ring of competition lurks the world's number one fast food restaurant. They are test marketing McPizza!

Grounds for War

Pizza is not the only battleground. The biggest players in the coffee market have been going after each other for over a decade. 55% of all American households serve up at least one piping hot cup each day. Maxwell House and Folgers are fighting for these so-called profit pots. Its a 3.5 billion dollar market where profit is generally wasted on advertising.

Phillips Morris, the parent of Maxwell House, upped the advertising ante to over one million dollars in annual advertising expense. Proctor & Gamble, the other parent followed suit. Their corporate aggressiveness in pursuit of market share wiped out any chance for profit. A commodity which produces profit at about a penny a cup cannot achieve much profit success when the war is only being fought over taste and price. Both cost money. One requires advertising to get the message across while the other inevitably leads to unwise price-cutting.

Their answer?

Forget the customer. Reduce the amount of coffee per can, keep the price the same, and fight on!

Charging Into War

Plastic isn't a precious metal. It isn't glamorous like gold or as functional as silver. It isn't traded in the commodities market either. Yet it is clearly worth fighting over. Just ask the folks at VISA, American Express, Master Card, Discover, AT&T Universal, and Diner's Club. Or pose the question to J.C. Penney, Speigel, or any of the baby Bells who are all considering ventures into the plastic wars.

Still not satisfied? Ask the airlines, sports teams, and service organizations who want their names and logos embossed on the affinity cards issued by the credit card companies.

The average American carries three such cards and there are more cards in circulation than the U.S. population. Examine the Citibank balance sheet. It reflects an annual take of $3.6 billion in credit card interest and pocket change of $500 million in annual card fees.

Is this market worth fighting over? You can bet your last dollar on it.

Those who issue credit cards make money three major ways:
1. The annual fees that are charged to customers.
2. The interest earned on unpaid credit balances.
3. The charge assessed to merchants on each purchase.

When new issuers enter the crowded field they attempt to achieve market share by offering improvement in one of the three categories. That's what happened when AT&T Universal joined the battle. With its initial offering of "free for life" cards it quickly attracted willing consumers.

In addition, AT&T offered instant credit on disputed charges and promised to be the ombudsman for customers in these disputed cases. Universal attacked the industry on both price and service.

According to the *Nilson Report*, credit cards produce 70% of the net profits for large bank card issuers, such as Citibank and Chase Manhattan. It is understandable that the areas where banks least want to battle is price. They can't afford it.

Cards are used approximately 2.3 times a month. With over one quarter of a billion cards in circulation, the dollar potential is substantial. The days of growth at home are gone because those who would qualify for a card already have one. Look for the war to continue to move into the expanding global marketplace.

None of the competitors has lost their zeal for charging into war.

Reading About War

The two largest national chains of discount bookstores are doing head-to-head battle in the Los Angeles area. The area is a lucrative market and both chains are intent on seizing it. Crown Books Corporation which operates 255 stores nationally and Bookstop, Inc. which has 46 are the two competitors. In 1991 these two companies built eleven stores in the Los Angeles area.

For now, there appears to be room for both competitors. That hasn't stopped the slings and arrows however. Bookstop took to the radio to promote its new operations. Crown answered with television ads that promote the company's low cost strategies. Bookstop discounts its bestsellers by 33%. Customers can also purchase a "People's Choice Card" which provides for an additional discount. Crown's discount for the same material is set at 40%. No cards or memberships are required at Crown stores. In fact, the company's founder finds the discount card concept distasteful. Of course, this just heightens the competition between them.

Independent bookstores haven't gone away. Independents still represent one third of the nation's bookstores. One of the Los Angeles independents that is watching the warring factions closely is Dutton's. The arrival of the new kids on the block has changed how Dutton's does business. New fiction books are now discounted 20%, non-fiction by 10%.

Who is winning the bookstore wars? Right now it is the consumer. They are being treated to better selection, lower cost, and a pleasant atmosphere for shopping.

New Markets

The United States is the largest consumer market in the world yet many companies have to look to foreign markets for success. If the national market isn't expanding (some call it maturity) then companies have to look elsewhere to improve market share.

The third largest ice cream maker in the U.S. is looking toward Mexico and Japan for market expansion. The four hundred fifty stores in Mexico's Palatas Manhattan chain of ice cream parlors plan to distribute Blue Bell products.

Compared to the efforts of Italian and French designers who have pursued the U.S. market for many years, the description of U.S. clothiers as the OPEC of the apparel industry seems aptly put. They have been slow to exploit the global markets.

Despite the fact that the home field for U.S. clothing designers is the world's largest and most competitive, the only one who has gone global in any decisive way is Ralph Lauren. Others like Blass and de la Renta will be forced to follow.

It is difficult to notice but the U.S. denim market isn't blue heaven anymore. Guess what is providing most of the sales growth for the denim giant, Levi Strauss: foreign sales. If you leave your Levi's at home there is no need to worry. If you're in Europe, Latin America, Canada, or Asia you easily replace them.

New markets. Crowded markets.

Japan's H-II commercial rocket will be airborne by the mid 1990s. Commercial rocket launches can really be called "big" business. The current cost of one launch carries a 75 million dollar price tag. Japan will join the U.S., China, Soviet Union, and the 13 nations in the European Space Agency (ESA) in launching satellites for other countries.

Remember the number of times you've heard a discussion on the value of teamwork. Consider the twelve member team forming in Europe under the moniker of the European Common Market (ECM).

The Common Market, which officially began late 1992, will eliminate trade barriers that block imports and exports to and from the rest of the world. The ECM will undoubtedly open up new opportunities for U.S. and Pacific Rim countries and open another vital battleground for corporate warriors in search of another conquest.

What's going on is already known **if** we can just figure it out. There are corner-office executives who understand that. Unfortunately, there are still too many who won't get it until it's too late. Possibly one way to convince them of the changing face of competition might be the simple admonition that

The ticket for the late train is always the most expensive.

Thinking Profits

In the middle of the high stakes poker game of new markets, new products, global competition, and a single world economy rests **profit**. Profit forms the foundation of corporate competitiveness and remains the core of the free enterprise system. The song from the Broadway play *Cabaret* says it best, "Money makes the world go round."

Competition is all about profit. Without profit warriors cannot compete. Profits are an expression of corporate risk in the same way that wages are an expression of the effort of workers. In the highly unpredictable environment of competition, profits are the road to corporate financial stability.

Corporate attitudes toward profits can substantially influence the extent to which they are achieved. There is more than one road to a solid bottom-line.

Diversification, acquisition, capitalization, sell-offs, down-sizing and multinational expansion define an "all in the numbers" approach. Improvements in innovation, quality, service, and research and development represent qualities of a second kind.

Global competition is more than just product competition. It is competition to find the best way to arrange people with the machines they use. It is integration of concepts like self-management and empowerment into the traditional way of doing things. Global competition is about **teams**, **partnerships**, and **coalitions**. It is about shared ideas and common goals.

In the new environment, structures, processes, systems, and characteristics of the managerial infrastructure, such as attitudes and beliefs, are also competing against each other in the world marketplace.

Sustained profits are not in the cards unless attention is given to all the factors that define competition. A global war is on. Only the smartest of warriors will survive.

1974 was a long, long time ago in a land far, far away!

19

The Land of Lean

"Just as mass production swept away craft production, the new lean production is going to sweep away mass production."

James Womack

Painful Adjustments

When you're young you think you'll live forever. The "immortality" of youth encourages risk taking with wild abandon unlike any other time in life. As you get older you realize that nothing lasts forever, **particularly you**.

When people get older, health and physical fitness take on greater importance. Giving these matters necessary attention improves the odds of living a longer, more satisfying life. Weight loss centers, fitness facilities, diet drinks, workout videos, and diet books are just a few of the contemporary tools of health and physical fitness.

Still Americans are stressed out and fatter than ever. The $32 billion diet industry isn't in good shape either. Sixty-four percent of Americans are at least 30 pounds overweight but only one in four is on a diet. In 1986, 65 million Americans were on a diet. By 1991, the number "taking it off" was down by 28%.

Despite the wish for good health and a youthful appearance, talk and good intentions are more likely than measurable results. Americans spend more on health and physical fitness than any other country in the world yet slimming down and staying healthy remain costly, illusive goals.

While individuals have enjoyed only modest success in becoming lean, corporations are on a tear. **Mass is out. Lean is in**. Downsizing, restructuring, and flattening define how to get there. Lean defines being there. Lean is being achieved in record numbers. Corporate America is shedding its excess weight.

Corporations are forced to change because they have to face the harsh realities of the market-place everyday. The new competitive realities are forcing corporate America to make painful adjustments. One of the adjustments is called **downsizing**.

The roll call of companies that have enlisted in the downsizing brigade are a Fortune 500 Who's Who. Today's business environment is so unforgiving that drastic steps are the only hope for many firms. Despite cutting 3.5 million white and blue collar jobs during the 1980s, deep cuts in the corporate structure still continue.

Roll Call

In response to a market decline for products in their core business, Kodak announced elimination of 3,000 jobs in a corporate restructuring in their imaging, health, and chemical divisions. Another 7,500 position were eliminated two years earlier.

To make the company more focused and competitive, Compaq

announced a 135 million dollar restructuring which called for layoffs of 12% of their workforce. In real terms, the layoffs affected 1,400 of Compaq's 12,000 employees worldwide.

Reducing operating costs by one billion dollars over two years was the reason cited by DuPont in announcing elimination of over 1,000 jobs. The company utilized voluntary leave and early retirements to achieve the goal. The downsizing effort saved the company nearly 200 million dollars. In order to stay downsized, DuPont is also starting to buy rather than build all of its own technologies.

Telesis has offered early retirement incentives to achieve a 17% reduction in the company's management group. Of the company's 18,000 managers more than 3,000 were expected to accept the offer.

Merrill Lynch cut 4,000 positions from its marketing, planning, and accounting units. Brunswick cut its headquarters staff by 40%. Texas Instruments will eliminate 3,200 positions through early retirements.

The Boston Globe cut twenty managers. Time, Inc. cut eight percent of its 1,300 editorial slots. United Technologies Corporation will trim its corporate staff 25% in order to slash operating costs by 1 billion dollars.

World-wide IBM cut 40,000 jobs in 1992 on top of the 20,000 cut in 1991. The blue in "Big Blue" has taken on a very different meaning.

In some cases it isn't only jobs which are cut. A peek into the future is what U.S. Air provided when it announced it was cutting pay by 20% and some medical benefits to offset operating losses. For those who retained jobs in the downsized workplace this could prove to be an ominous sign.

Corporations aren't the only ones on a diet. The City College of San Francisco has reduced its number of administrators from 71 to 46. The University of California expects 3,000 employers to retire early under its first early retirement offering.

And finally, one behemoth of government agencies is also downsizing. The U.S. Postal Service has sliced 37,000 workers. Near the end of 1991, Postmaster General Anthony Frank announced plans to trim another 47,000 workers by 1995.

With the 4.5 billion in anticipated savings, you'd think the cost of a 1st class postage stamp wouldn't have to go to 32 cents.

Before the year ended, 1991 easily won the label of "year of massive layoffs." 335,000 people who were employed as the new year began found themselves displaced before 1991 ended. The downsizing trend is a long way from finished.

If there is a light at the end of the tunnel, it's probably a train.

Protected Class

It wasn't too long ago that employees who held white collar jobs had guaranteed job security. In exchange for their loyalty to the company it was a reasonable expectation that the company would be loyal to them. It wasn't unusual for white collar employees to spend their entire careers with one company.

The rules have changed and white collar employees are just as vulnerable to job loss as their blue collar counterparts. Some have even suggested that computers are replacing middle managers at a much greater rate than robots are replacing blue collar workers.

It is in the **middle layer** of the organizational pyramid where the carcass of traditional industrial America can be found. The structure that once held those who collected, processed, and passed information up and down the hierarchy are being smashed into oblivion by the computer.

This so-called user friendly device has become so efficient that top management has all the information that used to be supplied by those in the middle tier.

Not only does technology change the standards of competition it alters the way organizations structure themselves and it subsequently affects skill requirements and jobs. When the logic is extended you reach downsizing. And, hopefully, **downpowering**.

Consider that only slightly more than a decade ago there were 15% more middle managers worldwide than there are today. The modern corporation is being reinvented and the shake out isn't over yet.

Much of the downsizing is being done in the name of recession and changed market conditions, but the downsizing would have occurred anyway. Mass production has given way to the age of information. The new marketplace is causing organizations to rethink how they operate.

Top management is figuring out what doesn't work. The structures that worked when mass production and price were the two major considerations won't work any more. Behind the recession are **structural** problems that are being addressed, albeit too late. As a result, what is occurring can be described as chaotic downsizing. It looks like more of an accident than a plan.

After Eiji Toyota visited Detroit in the 1950s to see how American cars were made he went home with a goal of doing it better. Taiichi Ohno, a Toyota vice president invented the lean system, and Japan's corporations have been lean ever since.

Future American corporations will be wider **not** taller. There will be horizontal integration instead of the traditional integration up the vertical ladder. The layers that served corporate interests for nearly three-fourths of a century are giving away to more updated arrangements. Some have suggested that the **pyramid** is giving way to the **spider web**.

Discouraged

Downsizing has its costs. Not only does it cause a large number of displaced workers, it has created a whole new class of workers. Call them discouraged. According to the U.S. Department of Labor there are more than one million discouraged workers and the numbers are growing.

Take the case of one discouraged worker. Please meet Fred Dearworth. A Harvard graduate with over twenty years of management experience, he lost his job to (you guessed it) restructuring. After months of looking for employment, frustration caused him to throw up his hands in despair and turn his back on the labor market.

Oftentimes smaller businesses can pick up some of the slack of corporate downsizing but that isn't happening. The Fortune 500 companies only employ 15% of all workers so people like Fred Dearworth generally have viable options with smaller businesses. According to figures from Dun and Bradstreet 43,000 of these businesses failed during the 1st six months of 1991. This was an increase of 15,000 over the same period one year earlier. The safety net for displaced middle managers has a gaping hole in it.

Other alternatives for the displaced worker traditionally include entrepreneurial ventures. Even with more than 9 million small businesses, there is always room for a new idea or a better way. According to those who counsel with people already in the small business game, entrepreneurial ventures aren't a good option for most of those currently being displaced. Years inside the corporate structure have left them ill-prepared for life on their own.

Long-Term Lean

Understanding the **need** to be lean is not all that difficult. Most corporate logic leads to the bottom-line. If the bottom-line isn't secure, then the jobs that depend on it aren't secure either. Lean isn't about short term financial results. It is about **long term** survival and success.

An oil company found that for each dollar it was spending on employees it was spending an additional 33 cents on management costs. The reason? A ratio of one manager for each 5.8 workers. Mass production turned modern organizations into giant centipedes. Centipedes which moved slowly, acted timidly, and ignored important signposts such as quality, customer service, innovation, timeliness, consistency, and variety.

Much like McDonald's introduction of a new 91% fat free hamburger, organizations must provide a leaner structure and staff. This necessitates a movement away from tinkering and temporary solutions. It increases the need to move toward flatter more flexible organizations.

2 B Lean

The future is now. Lean is about reshaping the organization for the future. Lean operating environments remove "muda", the Japanese word for waste. When organizations shed their fat they are placing a bet on perfection. In the lean operating environment there is little margin for error. Everybody and everything must perform like a finely tuned instrument.

The City of Phoenix required its Public Works Department to bid against private garbage collection companies for the city contract.

The issue got messy when the DPW didn't win the contract. Only after trimming its staff did the Public Works Department get its garbage back.

Consider the 398 million dollar prize won by CompuAdd Corporation because the company is finely tuned. On a Friday the company learned that it would share in a Defense Department Contract for 300,000 desktop computers. Its production system had to be redesigned to accommodate the order. By Monday morning its entire manufacturing operation had been redesigned to handle the production obligations.

They won the contract, in part, because a year earlier they were able to meet a deadline set by the Defense Department during the Persian Gulf Conflict. CompuAdd employees worked around the clock to meet a mid-January deadline. They put their customer orientation in high gear and began delivery two weeks ahead of schedule.

CompuAdd's version of lean includes no secretaries or vice presidents. There are only frontline managers. Memos and electronic mail are not permitted. Communication among employees is expressed face to face.

Computer industry giants and **all** of the rest of us will be forced to adapt to the style of our challengers. Companies like GM, Sears, and IBM will have to become leaner, more flexibly focused, customer oriented, faster to market, and service driven if they hope to regain market prominence.

They might keep this updated childhood nursery rhyme in mind:

> *Jack Sprat could eat no fat*
> *His wife could eat no lean*
> *Mrs. Sprat is no longer seen!*

In a lean environment organizations operate by a different set of rules. People, process and structure change.

In a lean operating environment there are fewer people left to do the work. The amount of human effort increases. Lean elevates the old standard, "People make a difference," to a number one hit.

Lean leaves less people to process information, produce goods, create new products, ensure quality, conduct research, or provide service. Lean requires major improvements **simultaneously** along several important dimensions.

Lean increases the need to share information. It brings reality to terms like empowerment, self-management, autonomy, and teams. Lean demands constant emphasis on training and retraining. The MIT Commission on Industrial Productivity concluded that successful organizational practices are accompanied by human resource policies that promote continuous learning.

Lean has even expanded the level of techno-talk. Lean has provided Just-In-Time (JIT) inventories which converge production with market readiness. Six Sigma is the statistical representation of the new quality standard. Zero inventory and zero defects are two of today's major process goals.

In the land of lean there is no room for the grim reaper. Ideas cannot be discounted or thrown away. Competition requires that **every** idea be considered. In the land of lean a problem belongs to **everyone** and so does the solution.

The Payoff?

Peak performance, competitive edge, and proactive winning organizations are what lean is all about.

Lean will continue to change the way management conducts its business. Management will be less a science and more a practice. The adjustments in modern organizations will continue to be painful.

Slimming down and staying healthy may be illusive goals for individuals, but organizations will have no other choice.

Welcome to the land of lean!

Part III

Managing Back

20

Here's Waldo

"If I have seen further it is by standing upon the shoulders of giants."

Sir Isaac Newton

Waldo-Mart

Sam Walton opened his first Wal-Mart in Rogers, Arkansas in 1962. What followed over the next 30 plus years is nothing less than a Cinderella story. Actually, it is more like Rumpelstiltskin's wish— spinning straw into gold.

Wal-Mart's success is even more staggering when considering what happened to other discount chains during the same three decades. None of the top ten discounters in 1962 are still in the field. Only half of the top 20 discount chains that existed in 1980 are still operating. But Wal-Mart sticks to its spinning and turns out much more than glitter.

Business Month named Wal-Mart one of the year's five best companies in 1982 and again in 1988. *Fortune* magazine listed Wal-Mart as the ninth most admired corporation in 1988 and by 1991 the listing had gone up to number four.

In January of 1991 Wal-Mart became America's number one retailer and boasted sales of almost $33 billion. As if acknowledging its new found status, Wal-Mart celebrated by opening 36 stores simultaneously in the month of January. If you had invested $1,000 in 1962, your money today would be worth well over $1 million.

There are 1,970 Wal-Mart stores across the U.S.A. That number does not include 419 Sam's Clubs or the 70 Wal-Mart Super Centers.

Waldo can be found in many pieces of Wal-Mart's success story.

Sam Walton rejected the conventional thinking of his day that a discount store could not be successful in a community of less than 50,000. His whole strategy was to focus on small town markets in the South and Mid West bringing discount prices to low and middle income Americans.

Although, not a particular fan of technology, he realized that it had tremendous discounting potential and surrounded himself with operational specialists who knew how to apply it. Wal-Mart is a pioneer in application of the universal product code and developed the most sophisticated inventory control system in the business. Twenty seven distribution centers allow direct ordering from manufacturers. Numerous company planes and a six-channel satellite television system allows communication with each store.

Wal-Mart management has been brilliant. Managers visit stores two or three days a week. And the top 100 managers meet weekly to pour over inventory lists. Department heads enjoy a wide span of empowerment that can include up to 30 departments. Each manger operates like a entrepreneur. Through detailed feedback they know their costs, margin of markup, overhead, and profit margin. They also have a series of financial incentives. Most of the employees are members of the profit sharing plan and there is even a "shrinkage bonus," which keeps employee theft to less than half of the national average.

Wal-Mart keeps its more than 500,000 employees highly motivated by giving them information, involvement, opportunity for input, and a piece of the rock. There are no employees, there are only "associates." Suggestions are earnestly sought and utilized. Each store has an official greeter who welcomes and tries to assist customers. This was an employee idea that was adopted corporation wide. The key pronouns at Wal-Mart are "**we**," "**us**," and "**our**." President David Glass quotes originator Walton frequently. "There are no superstars at Wal-Mart. We have average people operating in an environment that encourages everybody to perform above average."

Administrative and other general costs are really **lean**. With national competitors spending about 26% of gross sales, the Wal-Mart figure is 16%.

The ultimate beneficiary of all of this is the customer. Sam Walton believed that every associate should walk up to a customer, look him straight in the eye, and ask with friendliness and sincerity, "How may I help you?"

Customers come in for the "everyday low prices" and they are not disappointed. Wal-Mart prices reflect a 24% gross margin, which is the lowest in the business. Number two competitor, K-Mart, has a 27% gross margin and since K-Mart has 2,200 stores versus the 1,800 Wal-Mart stores, overall profits are 2.7% higher at Wal-Mart.

Wal-Mart's productivity loop improves steadily. More efficiency equals even lower prices and the Super Centers mean more lean.

Wal-Mart's real success is its **culture**. By representing the consumer with power buying and rock bottom prices, its aggressive hospitality has won millions of fans.

Wal-Mart plans to expand into the far west and the northeast. **Think about it**. Already America's number one retailer, Wal-Mart hasn't located in places with the most people, yet. $32 billion in 1990; $40 billion in 1991; $55 billion in 1992 and $62 billion in 1993. Wal-Mart is eyeing $125 billion by the year 2000.

McWaldo

The year was 1948. The McDonald brothers (Maurice and Richard) had operated a successful octagonal glass car-hop restaurant since the early 40s. The restaurant catered to teenagers who came in droves.

Although their gross sales reached almost a quarter of a million dollars in 1947, the McDonald brothers were not happy campers. The turnover rate for employees was high, new competitors had entered the game, and the car hops were young and energetic so they attracted mostly their teeny-bopper friends. One consequence was a high loss of silverware.

In the fall of 1948 the McDonald brothers did a strange thing. They closed their restaurant for 100 days, relegated the car-hops and converted their windows for customer **self-service**. By converting to paper plates and flatware, they eliminated the need for dishwashing and dealt with their major theft problem. The menu was cut from 25 to 9 items that were precooked. This allowed greater speed, higher volume, and lower cost. When the restaurant opened the old 35¢ hamburger was history. The new speedy system allowed a profit at a price of 15¢.

Within a year a new level of success had been achieved. The market switched from teenagers to adults and families.

In 1955 the entrepreneurial genius Ray Kroc opened the first franchise operation in Des Plaines, Illinois. The rest is history.

By 1988 nineteen of every twenty Americans had eaten at least one meal at a McDonald's restaurant in the past year. McDonald's sold 32% of all hamburgers and over one-fourth of all french fries sold in the U.S.A. The golden arches were responsible for 17% of the restaurant visits and commanded more than 7% of all the money Americans spent eating out. There were 10,000 McDonald's outlets. Company revenues were $5.5 billion.

In 1990 McDonald's was responsible for one-half of all the hamburgers sold and had cornered 25% of the fast-food market. They served 18 million Americans a day and took in $6.6 billion. If you had put $2,250 into McDonald's in 1965, it would have been worth $1 million in 1993. Today with 14,400 restaurants in 70 countries, McDonald's is simply the top food chain in the world!

How did they do it?
Their success includes speed, quality, consistency, the application of technology, customer-centered service, and the determination to make continous improvements.

No one has done a better job at product innovation than McDonald's. The innovations include the Big Mac in 1960s, the Egg McMuffin in the 70s, Chicken McNuggets and pre-packaged salad in the 80s, and the 91% fat-free McDonald's Deluxe of the 1990s.

The firm has addressed education on a scale seldom seen. At its 80-acre Oak Brook, Illinois Hamburger University, trainees undergo an intensive two-week course. One exit level test is to assembly a 60-part milkshake machine blindfolded.

One Ray Kroc progressive idea that proved potent was his attitude toward franchising. The usual practice was for the parent company to sell large area franchises. The areas would be subdivided into various districts and a lot of middle managers skimmed royalties amongst the layers. In the Kroc style franchising the **layers** of bureaucracy were bypassed.

Piloting has been another tool that McDonald's has utilized well. McDonald's has experimented with more than 150 menu items. Recent tests have concentrated on such items as baked apple pie, pizza, McHoagies, and fruit and vegetable McSticks.

The guardians of the golden arches have also done a superb job in analyzing and utilizing major societal trend line changes. As the two-career couple emerged, McDonald's opened for breakfast. As more customers started to eat off premises (only 1 in 4 in 1982, but 3 out of 5 in 1990), McDonald's responded with double windows, one to pay and one to pick up.

As customers became more concerned with health and diet, McDonald's was the first fast-food chain to introduce its McLean Deluxe in April 1991. The new burger contains only 9% fat, about one-half of a regular hamburger. The introduction was not an accident. In August of 1990 McDonald's executives met with researchers at Auburn University where the low-fat burger procedure was discovered. They began testing McLean in November 1990 and **in only nine months**, they took the idea from drawing board to the national market.

A second trend line garnering golden arch attention has been the environment. In November 1990 McDonald's announced that it would phase out its polystyrene foam clamshells because McDonald's customers were not comfortable with such containers.

On a third front, McDonald's responded to a national two-year recession by introducing its "value menu." The discounted prices boosted restaurant traffic by 2% in the spring of 1991.

With the $74 billion fast-food industry being somewhat stagnate in the United States, McDonald's is redesigning itself for future growth.

Although that thought may strike some like throwing out successful Classic Coke, potent new thrusts have re-invigorated McDonald's over the past four years.

First, recognizing that restaurant development costs went up more than 60% between 1985 and 1990, McDonald's reduced both the size and cost of its new restaurants. What formerly cost $1.6 million now costs $1.1 million. Consequently, they can open 4 new outlets for the former price of 3.

Second, McDonald's has beefed up its foreign openings. Now operating almost 5,000 stores (double that of 5 years ago). There are two new foreign units to each domestic.

Third, Waldo Burger has begun to operate "satellite sites" at hospitals, universities and air lines. One recent arrangement with Wal-Mart will convert 60 snack bars.

There is massive room for growth during this decade. But Michael Quinlan, the 52-year old McDonald's chairman, is not about to give up on the home front. He says that he will do "whatever it takes" to totally dominate quick service restaurants world wide.

And Quinlan is **passing authority down** the pipeline. In the old days an employee would have to get a manager's okay to replace a customer's spilled soft drink. Now that is an automatic. Quinlan, incidently, is the person responsible for the prepackaged salad introduced in 1987, which now provides 7% of total sales.

McDonald's does an excellent breakfast business and a high volume of business for lunch. Only 20% of its sales come after 4:00 p.m.

McDonald's is the answer.

The question: "Guess who will be delivering dinner?"

Waldo Mouse

The very mention of the word Disney evokes images of the land of enchantment itself. Best known to millions of Americans by way of its Anaheim, California Disneyland or Orlando, Florida Disney World, smiles come to faces, eyes light up, and you can almost hear "It's a Small World" beckoning in the background.

Actually, the Walt Disney company is composed of three major divisions: film, consumer products, and theme park-resorts. Michael Eisner became chairman and CEO of the company on 1984 and promptly "hi-hoed" off to work.

In 1984 the consumer product division did $110 million in volume. Six years later it was almost $600 million. In 1984 the movie division did a meager 3% of the Hollywood box office business. In 1990 it was the box office leader. Under Eisner's leadership the theme park business boomed and the accompanying hotel volume rivals the size of the Ritz-Carlton chain.

In 1984 Disney's annual revenue was $1.5 billion. In 1994 it was $8.5 billion.

How does Disney do it?

By way of focus. Let's single out Walt Disney World.

When the theme park opened on October 1, 1971, there were 10,000 people on hand. If you think that's good news, please realize in the last 20 years that number represents the slowest day. Each year more than 25 million people jam the grounds and spend more than $2 billion. Despite the huge crowds, exit polls show that the satisfaction rate remains unreasonably high.

Success at Enchantment Land begins when the customer arrives and parks his car in Snow White, section ten or Prince Charming, section four. "Our business," explains Eisner, "is **exceeding** customer expectations."

The 32,000 employees are all referred to as **cast** members who are putting on a show. Disney World has become the largest non-governmental employer in Florida.

With all the exhibits, gadgetry, and innovations, the intent is clearly not only to surprise, but actually to delight each and every customer. Disney World has become the world's leading fireworks enterprise, spending more than $30,000 a night.

A new Disney-MGM Studios theme park was added to the property in 1989 going beyond Disney characters. The theme park stresses themes from more than a dozen non-Disney movies, such as *Tarzan* and the *Wizard of Oz*. 1989 also saw the opening of the Typhoon Lagoon complete with seven-foot surf making capabilities.

Disney World has made impressive use of high technology and may be one of the world's leading examples of the I-T-A chain. Disney has applied for many of its own patents and has made remarkable use of new laser and fiber optics technology. The animation studios have a hot new property, CAPPS (Computer-Assisted Post-Production System). The technology digitizes drawings for colorization and movement reducing both the time of production and cost for cartoon production. Imagineering at Disney has also come up with audio-animatronics. Thus a robot can be made to look and sound sensationally realistic. The three divisions of Disney not only allow, but expedite an I-T-A chain reaction whereby a property is created, turned into product and then featured and reinforced by becoming a new attraction at the theme parks. Each piece generates more customers and starts the process anew.

From the customer's point of view, the attractions such as Space Mountain, Pirates of the Caribbean, or the Haunted House rank a distant third beyond the friendliness of the employees and the cleanliness of the entire theme park.

And how about those long lines (after all, isn't that the number one consumer complaint in America?) Disney has taken line management to a new art form. Posted waiting times are two to three times the actual waiting time so that customers are pleased that it went so quickly. Also, Disney keeps the lines moving all the time. As long as the lines are moving, does it really matter if you are only in a "preride waiting area."

Ever wonder why in all this bog land, mosquitoes are not a constant customer annoyance? Disney World is debugged by nocturnal spraying.

Disney University is a must for all cast members. Three days of motivational classes greet every new employee and refresher courses will come from time to time. What do the employees learn? "To help people do the hard work of helping other people have fun," according to director Valerie Oberle.

Part of the enchantment at Disney World is staying at one of the many beautiful hotels on the property. That's another big part of the Disney magic money machine. Whereas average hotels might have a 60% occupancy rate, Disney hotels run at better than 92%.

While it is true that the growth rate of Disney over all has fallen to about 15%, and Euro Disney was a severe misstep, the magic continues. If you had invested $1,000 in 1984, it would be worth $12,000 today.

"It's a small world after all...."

Hair's Waldo

Supercuts Inc. was begun in 1975.

The franchise was based on a new concept in cutting hair. Instead of a barber shop cutting men's hair or a beauty shop catering to women, the new unisex shop would serve **both**. In addition to the unisex audience, focus would also be on stressing a basic haircut, high quality, consistency, and an affordable price. Customer convenience was highlighted by having the shop open 80 hours a week, location in strip shopping malls, and the fact that customers did not have to make an appointment.

From the employee (stylist) point of view, "Supercuts does not force you to develop a clientele and then earn a commission. You immediately become an employee including benefits such as vacation and holiday pay. There are also numerous wage incentives and bonuses."

A dramatic growth and success of Supercuts has actually been achieved in two waves. Wave A occurred in the first 12 years. In 1987 Supercuts had 500 locations and revenues of $126 million. Major friction between the franchisees and franchisor reached its climax in the fall of 1987 when Supercuts was sold to a group of investors who promptly named Betsy Burton as the new chairperson and CEO.

Over the next four years the franchise added 100 locations and boosted its revenues by more than 35%.

Two questions: (1) How does Supercuts do it? (2) How did Betsy Burton revitalize the franchise?

From the very beginning Supercuts has looked at its operation from its customer's point of view. The shops are clean, neat, and the stylists are friendly. More stylists work during peak hours to cut down on long periods of waiting. The franchise realizes that customers have a choice whether to come in the first time or to come back. Repeaters are the central core of the business.

Management at Supercuts is not an afterthought. Alan Sager heads up the $12 million volume 46 franchises in Texas, Louisiana, and Illinois and says that he receives daily computer reports from every shop. "I know every day what has happened in every store," he says.

Each store manager is **really** the manager. They hire, develop, discipline, and fire. Every employee is evaluated three times a year and some evaluations take place monthly. Successful evaluations mean that you might get a December bonus.

Employees are told from the beginning that they can have a **career,** not just a job with the company. The career chain progresses from stylists to shift manager to assistant manager to apprenticeship to manager.

Training is an essential ingredient. Every new stylist, although already licensed, must participate in a week long training program where they learn how to cut a few basic styles by precise methodology. There are also continuing education opportunities that feature videos or consultants for styles that are "hot." Much of the training and update opportunities help develop a team atmosphere. All customers belong to the store not to a particular stylist. Quality and consistency are sought through expectations that stylists should have extremely infrequent "redos."

Incentives are a major part of Supercuts' culture. As Gary Grace, a 20-franchise supervisor in San Francisco, puts it, "I don't send memos; I send cash." There are numerous bonuses, contests, and awards to make each employee feel special if they are working hard.

All this makes the frontline more responsive and attentive to detail. Good morale means lots of ideas to do things better. Smiles come to stylists' faces and customers have a more enjoyable experience.

Down to the second question. How did Betsy Burton turn the franchise around?

With a seven-point **action** plan.

First, she had to reunite the kingdom. Even before she accepted the CEO role, she met with the franchisees and agreed to enough demands to get them to drop their class-action law suit. She agreed to establish a Supercuts council made up of elected franchisee representatives and sweetened the pot by contributing corporate money to advertising.

Second, she reduced corporate staff by one-half and brought in her own management team.

Third, Burton put an end to over spending by bringing in a disciplinary cost justification budget.

Next, she left history at the door step and departed from the service only Supercuts twelve-year history by initiating product sales of Nexxus and Paul Mitchell shampoos and conditioners. This effort was a massive success and boosted franchise revenues by almost $1 million a month.

Fifth, she departed from tradition again, and offered customers more than a good $8 cut. For $11 you could get a shampoo and a cut, and for $16, a shampoo, cut, and blow dry.

The sixth step of the plan was to pump an additional half a million dollars into training. She selected a dozen of the company's most talented to share their creativity and talent.

Last, although many of the franchisees expected the new CEO to go for quick profits, she chose to reinvest for the long term. Consequently, current franchisees felt much better and new franchisees were possible.

By 1991, Betsy Burton had added 100 new stores and boosted franchise revenues from $126 to $170 million. Supercuts is not only a story of success, it has been a blue ribbon case study in turning a business around. In the summer of 1993, Supercuts operated 840 stores in 39 states and CEO David Lipson has announced plans to add another 200 in the Tri State New York metro area.

Waldough

The fall of the Berlin Wall. The end of the Soviet Union. Bet you thought the clandestine Cold War games were over.

Maybe not.

Welcome to the world of plastic. Defections, intrigue, back stabbing, legal wars, and bone crunching attacks. That's the world of plastic money: credit cards.

American consumers today owe more than $3 trillion. The average household pays more than $300 a month, almost one-fifth of the family income for consumer debt of all types. A large and growing chunk is plastic credit. In 1990 Americans owned an average of three credit cards for every adult in the country.

The king of the hill? Visa International.

In 1991 Visa owned more than half of the $660 billion world market. Total number of cardholders were up 16% for 1990 to 260 million. And even though times were tough in America in the first half of 1990, rent-a-car charges were up 12%, lodging up 9%, restaurants up 8%, and total domestic charges, 9%. The field of travelers checks (an item that many customers previously thought of as Karl Malden and American Express) was up an astonishing 22%.

In many ways the growth of Visa has mirrored the demise of American Express. Whereas Visa went from a 47% volume to a 50% volume of the world market between 1986 and 1991, American Express declined by the same five points from 22% to 17%.

This telling statistic was no accident.

Back in the mid 80s American Express moved away from its prestige clientele and aimed at a much broader spectrum. Visa executives such as President Charles Russell and U.S.A. chief executive officer Robert Heller, realized quickly that this presented a provincial plastic opportunity. They seized it.

In the 1980s there had been a vast differential between the cards. The status was quite likely earned by American Express cardholders since bank cards had restrictive spending limits and American Express cardholders had minimum income requirements even for its lowest ranking Green Card.

Visa executives realized that the reputation of American Express and its image was about to undergo major surgery. They decided to appoint themselves as chief surgeon.

Credit card profits are made in three generous proportions: fees for the cards, interest on unpaid balances, and merchant discount fees. Visa decided to attack American Express on the former and the latter front.

In the early and mid 80s American Express could demand more in the way of customer fees because of its accepted status, its stable of wealthy cardholders, and additional perks.

Visa executives opened a two-barreled sixteen gauge attack on this front. "Why pay $55, $75 or $330 for an American Express card when you could get the same or better deal from Visa for $50 or less?" The first bullet said Visa was not a blue-collar card. The second cartridge ricocheted that Visa was welcomed by more world-wide merchants than AX.

While this broad public scatter gun campaign was going on, the Visa marksman aimed his narrow rifle fire at merchants. "Why pay 3% to 4% or more to AX when you can pay as little as 1% to 2% to Visa?" they asked.

Both the customers and the merchants got the message. They opted for full services at a lower price. A Gallup Poll in late 1991 noted that customers said they used Visa almost five times as often as AX.

Visa executives are not satisfied with this recent scrimmage. They are aiming for much greater success.

How can they get it?

Untapped markets.

In the early 90s, Visa has entered the $160 billion healthcare markets by signing up 1,300 doctors, hospitals, dentists. In the field of fast food, they have added 1,500 units including McDonald's, Wendy's, and Arby's. More than 3,300 supermarkets have come on board. Corporate clients include Pillsbury and Goodyear. International growth is clipping along at 35%.

In 1992, American Express fired its CEO after a series of mishaps and public relations goof ups. The unkindest cut of all? The $1.4 billion Optima disaster, the largest loss for bad debt in credit card history.

Meanwhile, Visa International just keeps on truckin. Since 1990, the number of Visa brand cards has risen by 5 million and Visa card spending is up a hefty $100 billion.

As for the future, a top Visa executive just winks and says that 85% of all transactions are done with cash or check. "That's the market we're after."

Waldo's Pension Fund

TIAA-CREF is the New York based Teacher's Insurance Annuity Association-College Retirement Equity Fund that has more than $125 billion in assets.

TIAA-CREF provides insurance and portable pensions to 1.6 million educators. TIAA has provided a fixed income return since 1918 and is the fifth largest provider of life insurance in the nation. CREF began more than 40 years ago as the first variable annuity in America. In 1990 TIAA-CREF funds provided more than $30 billion in life insurance, benefits, and dividends. With the past 10 years TIAA's average compounding rate has been more than 10%. CREF's rate, during the same period, has been more than 14%.

Things weren't so rosy. Back in February 1987, when Clifton Wharton became CEO of the organization they were not.

To say there was dissatisfaction would be somewhat of an understatement. Complaints were numerous, loud, and multi-directed. TIAA-CREF was seen as a massive unresponsive and even non-caring behemoth. Mutual funds and other insurance companies wanted part of TIAA-CREF's goodies. One university tried to get the Securities and Exchange Commission to mandate more choices than the few the corporation allowed.

When Wharton came aboard, he listened, analyzed, and acted.

In six short years he turned the organization's products, services, attitude, culture, and image completely around.

Today's TIAA-CREF offers a broad range of choices from money market funds, bond funds, even social choice funds. Participants have flexibility to change their choice or withdraw a portion of their savings.

Telephone operators offer a greeting of "TIAA-CREF at your service."

Ask Clif Wharton what he did to turn things around and reinvent his corporation and you would find several key tools. First is **listening**. "You must first find out what the problem is."

Step two was to **ask penetrating questions**. "Why do we do that?" he would often say followed by, "Is there a better way we can do it?"

Wharton believed very strongly in his employees. How many businesses do you know that operate a $100 billion plus budget with less than 4,000 of them? Employee morale is strong with such things as bonuses and opportunity to truly participate. Much of that downpowering comes about through a management restructured to four profit centers passing down some of the responsibility.

Wharton has also been bullish on strategic planning. At a typical retreat, 30 new ideas for products and services were discussed.

Wharton went way out of his way to find and support new talent. He had a "shadow" program where up and comers with high potential worked with him.

When he left to become Deputy Secretary of State in 1993, Clif Wharton had taken TIAA-CREF to new heights during his tenure.

Late Senator Everett Dirkson of Illinois would have loved Clif

Wharton: "A billion here, a billion there. Pretty soon you're talking about real money!"

WALDOrola

Motorola Inc. was founded in 1928. Because they put radios in cars they linked motor with the last three letters of Victrola and conceived the corporate name. They went out of the car radio business in 1980. In 1993, Chairman Gary Tooker's company did $17 billion in business as sales jumped 27%.

The inventor of the walkie-talkie, Motorola today is a world-wide manufacturer of electronic hardware: semiconductors, automobile electronics, pagers, modems, cellular phones, and of course, two-way radios.

One of the first three winners of the Malcolm Baldrige Award in 1988, Motorola found the early 80s extremely rough terrain. They were in a maelstrom of Bermuda Triangle portions.

In the early 80s, Japan began dumping pagers and cellular telephones in the U.S. market. The corporation flexed its Washington muscle and in 1982 forced Japan to open its pager market. Four years later the wedge was created in the semiconductor Japanese market as well.

In the meantime Japanese competition played havoc with pagers and cellular phones. Motorola was knocked completely out of dynamic random access memory (DRAM) chip field. In 1986 Motorola reassembled Humpty Dumpty just as he was about to fall from the wall. But over the next decade, all the king's horses and all the king's men arrived at Motorola. Motorola has a reputation for **quality** that is envied world-wide. Zeal for **customer service** is second to none and is implemented in almost every parcel of modern management thinking described in this book.

The quality initiative began almost a decade ago when management announced a five-year plan to get a ten-fold reduction in product defects. The stakes have been rising steadily. Next came a 100-fold reduction goal, Six Sigma (3.4 defects per million). Most of the quality goals came about when Motorola management saw other companies with much higher **expectations** than their own. On one visit a Motorola representative observed a Japanese firm expecting a 200% improvement within the same time span that they were expecting 25%. To make matters worse the Japanese product was already superior before the improvement.

The Six Sigma campaign has been extremely successful. Products produced by Motorola in 1991 were a hundred times better than those in 1987. And they will get better in the future. The company goal is to reduce its rate of error ten fold every two years without sacrificing speed.

Customer service has been an essential focus since 1986. Managers visit customers regularly and solicit customer opinions through surveys and field audits. The complaint hotline allows direct access for service satisfaction. Customer report cards for each and every product line can make the difference of bonus or no bonus to company sales personnel.

Motorola has poured millions into employee **training** for all of its more than 100,000 employees. Currently it spends more than $60 million a year in actual cost on education and another $60 million for lost work time. Education is a key component of the Motorola culture. Employees are expected to analyze and fix problems. There also is a major emphasis on self directed work teams.

Research and development at Motorola is committed to the long term. Two of their recent developments are the MicroTAC cellular phone of Star Trek communicator similarity and the world's first wristwatch pagers reminiscent of Dick Tracy or Captain Midnight.

In March of 1994, Motorola unveiled Envoy to the world. Weighing under two pounds, this hand held wireless communicator has a built in modem. You can tie into Internet, view your E-Mail or send a fax.

Creative borrowing and concern for **speed** have been two other areas for corporate success. One recent success story was **Operation Bandit**, which scoured the world looking for manufacturing short-cuts. The results were impressive. In 18 months **Operation Bandit** reduced the manufacturing time for custom ordered pagers from 27 days to less than 2 hours. Two-way radios that used to take 18 months are now processed in less than 30 days. Cellular phone manufacturing has gone from 15 months to 6.

Collaboration and **team** design engineering are also paying great dividends. The MicroTAC pocket slim phone has only 400 parts, about one-eighth as many as Motorola's first portable phone. Less parts mean less potential error as the completely integrated manu-facturing process feeds production along. State-of-the-art robots integrated with downpowered workers allowed production in 2 hours instead of the 40-hour previously required manufacturing time.

Motorola has also pushed its suppliers regarding quality and ser-vice. As a result suppliers have gotten better and fewer. The list has been reduced to about 400.

What has happened to Motorola over the last ten years is nothing less than a complete make-over. As you can see it is anything but cosmetic. And the world's leading manufacturer of pagers and cellular telephones continues to invent: lighter, cheaper and easier to use all at a rate doubling annual sales.

Motorola's goal?

To make every product right the first time, every time, and to do it better, faster, and cheaper.

WALDOcocca

After a brush with bankruptcy in 1980, Chrysler Corporation rang up five straight years of billion dollar profits. Stock value during this period went from about $3 a share to $100 a share, allowing for splits. Chrysler Chairman Lee Iacocca earned the nickname of "the cardiac kid" and became a national hero.

But things seldom stay the same and by 1990 Chrysler was stumbling.

Some diversification efforts had been unproductive. Its best selling mini-vans and jeeps acquired new competitors and Chrysler's K-cars had stayed long past their prime. As a matter of fact, there were gaping holes in Chrysler's offerings. After closing the Detroit plant that assembled the sub-compact Omni and Horizon, Chrysler had no small car in its lineup. On the other end of the spectrum, Chrysler had ceased production of its larger models. Its designs were out of date. The jeep and mini-van lines were its bread and butter.

To make matters worse, Chrysler had a large underfunded pension liability, and also ran into some major problems in the ultra-drive transmission in its 1991 models. The Big Three lost $5 billion in 1991. One-fifth of that was Chrysler's.

If this is so, what on earth would make Chrysler Waldo material?

The answer! Chrysler has embraced fundamental change in the past four years. Change that has transformed this poor 3rd sister into a Cinderella story.

Although there were some extremely critical months to survive during 1992, Chrysler has revamped and transformed itself over the past few years. In 1992, the profits were almost $1 billion. In 1993, over $2 billion. By 1995, the transformation will be complete.

To begin with Chrysler has become **lean**. Over a four-year period, from 1991 to 1994, Chrysler reduced its annual operation cost by $4 billion (16%). One in four white-collar workers are no longer present. Eleven layers of management have been reduced to nine. Thirty-six vice presidents and above have been reduced to twenty-three. Even the Chrysler board has undergone surgery from 18 to 13.

On the blue-collar side, it took 6,000 workers to turn out 1,000 units a day in 1989. By 1994, half that many.

In 1992 Chrysler unveiled its Viper, a sexy-looking Dodge two-seater. Although you would naturally think of speed when comparing the new $50,000 model to a $65,000 Corvette, Viper made speed history in an entirely different way. Chrysler brought the Viper from laboratory to production **in only three years**. That is about 60% of the normal U.S.A. five-year implementation span.

Even more significant than the production lapse time, Chrysler used Viper to learn much more efficient techniques that will be implemented in its revolutionary new development stadium.

On October 15, 1991 Chrysler unveiled its sleek and sprawling new technology center. The more than three million square foot, four-storied structure is located on 500 acres 30 miles north of Detroit. In every respect it represents the cornerstone of Chrysler for the 1990s. It is here that they hope to build the **best** vehicles in the world.

By 1994 seven thousand employees from 24 different locations worked in the new center. For the first time in history, product design, engineering, manufacturing, procurement and supply, sales and marketing, and finance are housed under one roof. The massive $1.1 billion structure is a modern, well-equipped technology center with state-of-the-art refinements such as a scientific test facility, an aerodynamic wind tunnel, electromagnetic compatible facility, environmental test center, power train test cells, noise vibration and harshness facility, and a 1.8 mile evaluation road.

It is here that Chrysler is spending the majority of its $16 billion five-year product plan. By 1994 Chrysler had introduced not only the all-plastic body Viper, but a new line of LH automobiles, a PL subcompact line, a new JA compact line, and a new line of mini-vans and trucks. Its LH family sedans, the Dodge Intrepid, Eagle Vision, and Chrysler Concord, received "Automobile of the Year" honors, as did the Chrysler Cirrus in 1995.

The new center presents a complete **transformation** by Chrysler. The corporation is doing nothing less than fundamentally changing the way it does business.

The new Chrysler culture made possible by the CTC is based upon close contact where the development sequence can be stepped up. With important players working side by side, decisions are made on the spot. The result: **simultaneous** engineering instead of waiting for each sequence. More than 6,000 engineers were assigned to one of four platform teams, not a specialty. The new time lapsed production process will trim a couple of years. In addition to the time savings there will be significant dollar savings. Production time can be reduced. Waste by almost 50%. Savings will amount to about $500 per car. While Ford and GM take $5 billion and five years to introduce a new automobile from concept to delivery, Chrysler spends $1.5 billion and less than three years.

Outsourcing also plays a major role in Chrysler's operations. General Motors has generally had about 30% outsourcing. Ford about 50%. Chrysler expects to go as high as 90% in the future. The philosophy is simple. Less capital outlay and less resultant risk.

The U.S. automobile industry creates directly or indirectly one out of every eight jobs in America amounting to more than 4% of our gross national product. It is highly encouraging even in a service economy to see these Waldo-like efforts.

With its $16 billion new product plans, breakthrough technology center, and transformational processing, Chrysler Corporation is again a money machine!"

Advantage Chrysler!

21

A Bag of Tools

Each is given a bag of tools,
A shapeless mass,
A book of rules;
And each must make—
Ere life is flown—
A stumbling block
Or a stepping stone.

R. L. Sharpe

In the 1990s the Zeitgeist Manager will have to utilize a new bag of tools. Tool kits and tool boxes designed for the Tayloristic mass production era are much more than out of style. Managers who try to guide the future with implements of the past will be free-falling toward oblivion.

Here are some of the tools that are required by Zeitgeist, the management essence of our time.

Utilizing Complaints

There was a time when complaints were simply relegated to the customer service department and placed on a low back burner. Past managers felt they only had to deal with those who **actually** complained. In many cases complaints were not even acknowledged, much less dealt with.

Today's Zeitgeist Manager looks at complaints as an **opportunity**. Why pay for advice from expensive consultants when you can get it from your customers free? If you really **listen** to a complaint, you have the **opportunity** to solve a problem.

Smart companies like Procter & Gamble make ubiquitous use of an 800 complaint line. Striker Corporation listened to problems regarding the use of medical beds. They changed the design of the bed based on complaints and became a multi-million dollar enterprise.

Outsourcing

Lean managers in the 1990s will have a smaller (core) workforce and go elsewhere (outsource) for changing needs.

When Texans voted to create a state lottery, Comptroller John Sharp was faced with establishing the equivalent of a new Fortune 500 company. Projected first year sales were one billion dollars. Unlike California and Florida who employ over a thousand workers for their respective lotteries, Texas employs less than 200. How? Sharp "contracts out" the printing and ticketing and other lottery tasks. The approach not only saves money, but stops Texas from building yet another bureaucracy.

Eastman Kodak recently entered into an outsourcing agreement with IBM. The new IBM-Kodak data center located in Rochester, New York will cut Kodak's data processing costs by 50%!

Outsourcing will continue to be one of the most frequently used tools of the 1990s. It was the source of a $6 billion industry in 1991 and reached $13 billion in 1994.

Benchmarking

Ironically, Frederick Winslow Taylor was a major proponent of benchmarking. In trying to move from craft to mass production, he felt that you ought to find the very best way of doing something and make that method the basis for mass production.

The U.S.A. became a world-class economic power during the 19th century by taking some of Europe's best benchmark methods and applying them. In the early 20th century such benchmark applications made us the best in the world.

For the past several decades we have been unwilling to scour the world for the best techniques. Although we freely acknowledge that California, Florida, and other states are bell weathers for demographic, social, and legislative change, we have been unable to admit that other nations may be doing it best. We need to shake that American pride and come to the realistic understanding that we can learn from the best practices elsewhere.

Alienation

German dramatist Bertold Brecht invented this device for use in the theater, but the **alienation effect** can become a major management tool in the 1990s.

Brecht became known for "thinking theater" by use of techniques that would remind the audience they were watching a play. His actors, for example, would break away from a scene to speak directly to the audience. Brecht's purpose was to distance the audience from the characters and events being portrayed.

Managers in the 1990s can learn a great deal from Brecht. Donald Peterson, former Ford Motor Company CEO, uses Brecht's device by asking a simple question, "Does anyone ever ask you how things could be improved?" And Richard Tanner Pascale urges managers to adopt a "restless, self-questioning quality."

Too often managers are overwhelmed by routine everyday occurrences. In asking how things can get better, they begin to have the realization that things **can** get better. One reality of the emerging 21st century is that you can't have breakthrough thinking, application, or action unless you begin with a breakthrough question.

Seek and Destroy

For much too long American managers have held the "let's not stop the assembly line for any reason" mentality. When something went wrong, it would be dealt with cosmetically and the assembly line would roll ahead.

Ford Motor Company, for example, utilized a shim when assembling its car bumpers instead of dealing with the real problem. A shim is a washer-like piece of metal that when added to the bumper makes it look like it actually fits the body of the car. This quick-fix mentality must be put to bed.

Our major competitor, Japan, has been using the **Five Whys** technique invented by Toyota's Taiichi Ohno since mid century. The technique is a systematic cause and effect intensive search where each and every error is traced back to its ultimate cause. Once located, a precise cure is found so that the error will **never** occur again.

Seek and destroy is an essential tool of the 1990s.

Delayering

Make no mistake, delayering of management levels is new **reality**, not a fad. Organizational build-up will not return with an upswing in our economy. **Pancake** now describes more than breakfast or makeup.

Just as the Franklin Mint has cut from six to four layers of management while doubling sales, the vast majority of large corporations have reduced their levels of management. DuPont, AT&T, Exxon, and Union Carbide have no plans to return to the bloated central offices of yesteryear.

Whether you follow the suggested **Rule of Six** or some other method, one new reality of the 1990s is that you do not need to, can't afford to, and will not be allowed to have a large number of indirect workers. For years they were considered essential. The truth is they are not.

Discounting

Discounting is simply cutting prices or selling for less.

Home Depot is able to sell for less by keeping its overhead to a minimum. Their stores are located in suburban areas where land is cheaper and double as a warehouse, since inventory is stacked over merchandise which is displayed on industrial looking racks.

Toys R Us, K-Mart, Price Club, Auto Giant, and many other examples of discounting success show the value of this technique by humbling such giants as Sears. Not satisfied with past discounting success, Wal-Mart is now trying to skip the middle man completely and buy directly from the factory. This is one of the ways that Wal-Mart stays in the forefront as America's number one retailer.

Discounting is going to be necessary in the future whether you are in education, government, service or manufacturing. You are going to have to deliver **more** to the customer **for less**.

Piloting

Piloting is the simple practice of doing something on a small scale before you implement it in a big way. The East Moline, Illinois John Deere Foundry learned this lesson the hard way. They purchased a multi-million dollar automated crane system that had to be shut down for a couple of hours every day because its computerized inventory system was not performing.

The problem at Deere is typical of many rush-to-the-floor advanced technology application efforts that backfired. Many companies were burned throughout the 80s because they didn't do needed homework by piloting that would make the technology injection take.

Austin Community College, an institution of 25,000 students in Austin, Texas, became 1 of about 100 institutions of higher education to install telephone registration. But having learned about some real disaster stories of other installation efforts, the management went the extra mile and piloted the new system for three semesters before making a total conversion.

Piloting is not a luxury. When taking advantage of new technology or some other innovation, it is a required first step that **must** be taken least you overstep and fall flat on your face.

Creative Borrowing

Creative borrowing means taking an idea from another process or product and applying it to yours.

Again, when it comes to borrowing from other countries, we are victims of our own success. After WWII we became both the Daddy Warbucks of research and development and the Orphan Annie of idea arrogance.

Much like a magician at Hollywood's Magic Castle, I ask you to pick a card. Which major industry could not have learned by creative borrowing in decades past: Automobiles? Textiles? Steel? Electronics?

History has obliged us with a smart slap on the face of the "Thanks,

I needed that," variety. Experience is **not** the best teacher even when it's in America. Somebody else's often is!

Horizontal Drilling

When the oil wells in the Texas Panhandle became somewhat depleted, somebody came up with a better idea: horizontal drilling. Horizontal drilling is the modern day equivalent of building a better mousetrap. By drilling in this manner, significant new oil outtakes were made possible.

How many years did we live with the old gas station oil changes and the long delays before Quick Lube? How many of us remember super market chicken before Pilgrim improved the size, color, and freshness?

Who remembers when you couldn't get eyeglasses in an hour? Much like Gramps in Steinbeck's *Leader of the People*, many of today's managers feel that "all the westerning" has been done— there's no place new to go.

Yet, people think of new ways to do things every day. Tomorrow's innovations will be new ideas **or** applications. It will also come from **horizontal teams** and **horizontal linkages**.

Incentives

An incentive is an inducement to buy a product or service.

Chrysler became the first American automobile firm to offer an air bag as an incentive to customers who were concerned about their safety. Now they are standard equipment.

H&R Block only recently introduced electronic rapid refund tax filing. For a fee of $25 your tax return is delivered to the IRS **instantly**. As another incentive, customers expecting refunds can get their money from H&R Block rather than wait on the IRS.

Federal Express has utilized incentives in a different way. Since many of its employees at the cargo terminal are college students, they now get paid by the job rather than by the hour. The result: the students get the job done **sooner**.

One of the most successful incentive programs has actually been a customer loyalty tool: the airline frequent flyer programs. Referred to by some as "funny money," some advertising executives think it is the greatest marketing strategy since "new and improved."

One recent poll of 520 travel agents nation-wide indicated that 80% of the passengers selected tickets on the basis on their frequent flyer program most of the time. No surprise then, that U.S.A. airlines owed more than $600 billion in funny money to their passengers by 1990.

Feedback

Oddly enough, the device of feedback can also be attributed to Frederick Winslow Taylor. At the turn of the century, he stressed how important it was for workers to be advised how they were doing.

Today's feedback goes much further than Taylor. Workers in the 1990s need to know as **much about** their product or service as management personnel in past decades. And tomorrow's worker will have to know even **more**.

The new pattern of work and work organization will require far more than assembling one item in one location for an entire day of work. Our workers will have to be able to work in teams, solve problems, and contribute to the organization's success.

Cascading Training

No doubt about it, the bulk of American workers have been trained poorly **if** at all. With most of the educational dollars focused on top management and only 8% on the millions of frontline workers, we still think as mass producers.

In addition to the changing nature of our organizations and our work patterns, we will be facing workforce shortages as our baby boomer population grows older and fewer Americans are in the labor force. As our workforce becomes leaner by design and by demographics, education will become a critical element in our new bag of tools. We will need to be better educated and put that education to good use.

Span of Empowerment
On the flip side of the delayering coin is span of empowerment. If the axiom is **less** layers of management, then the corollary must be **more** people managed by fewer people.

The new arrangement **cannot** be a growth in the span of control. Control exacts a specific limit on what lower levels of employees and frontline employees can achieve. If they are truly going to do more—and they will have to—they will have to have management of a new type in a new role that will empower and support these frontline workers.

The lean management necessitated in the 1990s will not allow a duplication of efforts by managers, supervisors, or the frontline worker. Whether a Rule of Six or not, the span of empowerment replacing the span of control must grow larger.

Intrapreneuring
In time past manufacturers, service organizations, government, and education would witness numerous individuals leaving the fold to become entrepreneurs. The trend in the 1990s will become **intrapreneuring**; that is, starting a new branch, business, or operation **inside** the organization.

The Wisconsin Public Service Electrical Utility in Green Bay, Wisconsin has constructed a simulated control training center to train nuclear plant operators. Over the first six years the program has generated $5 million in profit.

General Electric has a very successful Answer Center Consulting Service. In the past twelve years it has served more than 300 companies.

In Norwalk, Connecticut, Stew Leonard's Dairy has established its own university. Instruction is by two-hour segments of management training highlighting customer service. In the first year they took in $100,000.

The Bottom Up Chart

Some progressive companies and organizations have started to show the new found reliance on frontline employees via the design of their organization charts. Instead of starting at the top with the shareholders, CEO, or board of trustees, the organizational chart is inverted. Nordstrom and Embassy Suites are two of the early leaders in literally turning the organization upside down.

With the new realities of the 1990s upon us, the reverse pyramid is far more than a symbol. The supervisors and middle managers are in a supportive assistant role and the frontline work teams **actually** do it.

Bottom Up Interviews

If the action in the future is to be on the frontline and the supervisor, mid-management, and upper echelon management is to be more of an expeditor, then it makes sense that the hiring process should begin with interviews by peers. This is particularly important if the work is to be done by **self-directed** work teams.

If the team is to be rewarded on the basis of output, then the skills, personality, and ability to blend in with the rest of the team will become much more important. Discipline in the future will also be done much more by peer pressure.

Management Information Systems

Top managers of the 1990s will become heavily reliant on management information systems. Desktop computers that display daily baseline information in a clear and concise way will become the standard.

Managers will be able to look at these spreadsheets and "drill down" for more details on any particular item of interest. Daily inventory, units produced, or other such needed information will be at your fingertips.

Underpromising

In the 1990s customer perception may well be the most important ingredient for success. If you are to exceed customer expectations and actually surprise and delight, you might want to consider some advice from Richard Thalheimer, president of Sharper Image, and actually **underpromise**.

The Service Supply Corporation of Indianapolis, Indiana almost always succeeds in delighting its customers because of the massive inventory it carries. If you are looking for a particular fastener, bolt, or nut, general distributors would only have it 65% of the time. At Service Supply you've got it 19 in 20.

Just In Time

Just-In-Time process planning allows massive savings in terms of space and material or part inventory.

Levi Strauss, for example, has a new top-of-the-line computer system, "LeviLink," that allows customers to order and even pay electronically. The system allows Levi to implement just-in-time manufacturing and eliminates the need for large warehouses of fabric.

Luby's Cafeterias is a network of 144 restaurants located throughout the Southwest. By not utilizing a central warehouse, the speedy and inexpensive eatery has inventory of only four day's supply.

Deere and Company headquartered in Moline, Illinois has converted to cellular manufacturing techniques. This precise grouping of manufacturing machinery drastically cuts the overhead of work in process. Just-in-time delivery of combine cabs from an outsourcer saves almost $300 per unit.

Joint Venture

Sometimes competition means **cooperation**.

General Mills and Nestlē are involved in a joint venture that will take their products to Europe.

Corning Inc. has established several foreign joint ventures in fiber optics.

Domino's Pizza in tandem with American Telephone and Telegraph is testing a toll free telephone number for one-stop pizza shopping anywhere in the U.S.A. **Alcoa** is intertwined with numerous foreign partners attempting to reach ever growing Eurasian markets.

Certainly such ventures in local, state, and federal government efforts could be rich and lucrative. Education and higher education are also target rich environments.

Refocusing

H&R Block Inc. is a major advocate of this tool. Venturing beyond its core business of tax preparation has been a costly enterprise. In 1985 Block purchased Path Management Industries, a supplier of management seminars. Three years later Block sold the business and **lost** $15 million.

After another bout with a legal service business that didn't work out, H&R Block refocused on what it did best: tax filing at its 9,000 outlets.

When the IRS approved electronic filing in 1986, opportunity was knocking. In addition to its usual tax preparation fee, Block receives about the same amount to process early refunds and electronic filing fees. H&R Block has become a $1.1 billion company filing more than 14 million tax returns each year.

Gillette had a similar refocusing experience. Looking somewhat anemic in the mid 80s, Gillette refocused on the business it knew best and brought out the Sensor razor. In 1990, the Sensor's first year, it took 9% of the world market.

Goal Ratcheting

When you are ripe, you don't have to rot. The trick may be to recognize that you have achieved your goal and set a new and higher one.

Take a lesson from Peter Coors at the Golden, Colorado based Adolf Coors brewery. In 1990 Coors became the nation's third largest brewery cornering 10% of the market. Peter Coors, the great grandson of Adolf, was very articulate in putting past success in perspective. His goal for the 1980s was to be **number three** and growing.

His new goal?

In the 1990s he aims to be **number two** and growing.

Frosting

Just as Brecht provides sage, modern management advice from a theatrical perspective, Robert Frost weighs in with a pearl from poetry. In his famous poem, *Mending Wall,* Frost advises us that "something there is that doesn't love a wall, that wants it down."

So it is with management needs of the 90s.

When Cincinnati Milacron was faced with stiff foreign competition in the injection molding machine business in 1985, their rally cry became "tear down the walls." In days past engineers had designed injection molding machines behind a secluded wall. When they were finished, they threw the design over the wall. Manufacturing worked behind a new wall. Then the same separation pattern proceeded to purchasing and marketing.

Tearing down the walls allows Milacron to be the largest domestic manufacturer of injection molding machines in the U.S.A.

Process Mapping

Process mapping allows for visualization and simplification of any process. The goal is to examine every step necessary in making or doing something.

One General Electric plant mapped the entire process of making turbine shafts. The project took 30 days and an entire room.

With a goal of 100% maximum machine utilization, the map clearly articulated poorly arranged equipment. After adjustments GE shaved $4 million.

Ghost Busting

Tradition can be as warm and wonderful as viewed in *Fiddler on the Roof*. But in the 1990s you simply can't fiddle around with it.

When David Johnson became the head of Campbell Soup in late 1989, he did much more than sip the company's broth. He divested 20 plants, disposed of 1,000 workers, took unprofitable products off of store shelves, and put a clamp on the number of new product lines.

Although that is not the way Campbell's in the past has done business, it was the needed step. Campbell's net profits are up about one-third.

Sears still hasn't gotten the message. Although there are a few glimmers of hope, Sears is still clinging to an old middle of the road mid-price merchandising philosophy in its goods and services.

Lagniappe

Call it a baker's dozen, a small gift, a little bit extra, or just an overt expression of some additional appreciation, but in the age of surprise and delight lagniappe has truly outgrown the Louisiana territory.

Bank America's California Alpha account includes checking, savings, a line of credit, a unified monthly statement, and Saturday banking hours. On a recent founder's day celebration, Bank America bestowed 36 months of free checking accounts for that entire business day.

Epitaph Question

Probably one of the most important building blocks in the modern management tool box is the epitaph question. What does your organization want to be remembered for?

If you isolate the specific goal, your strategy for implementing it will emerge.

Perhaps your goal could be as simple and eloquent as that of Chrysler's Lee Iaccoca, "Our ambition? To be the best. What else is there?"

22

The Zeitgeist Manager

"We live and learn but not the wiser grow."

John Pomfret

Habits

What do nail-biting, knuckle-cracking, coin-jingling, hair-twisting, and foot-tapping have in common? Yes, they are all hyphenated words. But more importantly they are all habits. Habits occur so frequently they become automatic. They produce a consistent behavior which is duplicated over and over again. Some habits are copied. They are even passed from one generation to another. The practice of management is one such habit.

Management has been practiced in basically the same way for most of the 20th Century. It started with Taylor and it hasn't changed much since. Those who promote management as a science have done their best to complicate it though. They have put a new spin on old notions from time to time but significant workplace change **hasn't** really occurred. As the natural evolution of events take us from the industrial revolution to the information age, it is time to change the habits of management.

The habits of craft were not the habits of mass. The habits of the Agricultural Age were not the habits of the Industrial Revolution. Each era sets its own requirements and people and organizations adapt to them. Habits like wringing-hands, doodling, ear pulling, and chin rubbing may never change but management should be different. The way in which organizations are managed **must** change.

The challenge of the 21st century is to produce managers who are comfortable with their changing role. The old standards of management will be replaced by new traditions. The successful manager of the future will be a **helpmate** to workers. **Coach**, **teacher**, and **mentor** will be the new managerial descriptors. The relationship between management and workers will be based upon habits of the heart **and** habits of the mind.

In the movie *Wall Street* the Michael Douglas character, Gordon Gecko, bellowed the words, "This is your wake-up call, buddy-boy!" Public and private organizations everywhere are receiving their wake-up calls. The new operating environment is forcing necessary adjustments in the workplace. Those who understand the changing role of the zeitgeist manager will clearly leap-frog ahead of the competition.

Management Happens

There is not much that happens as often as management. It happens every minute of every hour of every day. It happens all over the world. It has even happened in space. It happens in small businesses and large multinational conglomerates. It happens at the neighborhood elementary school and in the British Parliament. It happens at New Pig, McDonald's, Gateway 2000, Nordstrom, and Chrysler. It happens at Citicorp, AT&T, Supercuts, and K-Mart. It happens in households, churches, and movie theaters. It happens everywhere.

More often than not management happens haphazardly. But it can also happen with careful consideration. Management happens through structure and rules. It can also happen through teams and freedom. Management happens with demands and deceptions. It can also happen with approval and praise. Management happens with threats. It can also happen with suggestions. Management happens corruptly, but it can also happen ethically. It happens whenever people join together to achieve a purpose — whatever the purpose happens to be. Sometimes it even happens with a little bit of luck.

Luck

Luck is an interesting word. It has only two faces, good and bad. Without good and bad, luck is an empty word. Sometimes luck has more to do with success or failure than smarts. When your luck is good, you succeed. When it's bad, you fail. In other words, people believe that you can do the right things and fail or do the wrong things and succeed. The early days of Hollywood illustrate the point.

Hollywood was once a town without glamour. Before the giant letters that spell H-O-L-L-Y-W-O-O-D even existed or before there was a Hollywood & Vine or Rodeo Drive, this southern California city received a bushel of good luck. It was wrapped with celluloid.

The original one reelers were described by their makers as "stupid little movies" and considered nothing more than a weird gimmick. No matter what the producers of one reelers did, the money just kept rolling in. No one had any idea about the enormous possibilities that films and those who starred in them had for unifying the country. Hollywood can best be described as a happen stance.

One who typifies how films and film making were viewed in the early days is Charlie Chaplin. Hollywood's luck was his good fortune. He came to Hollywood as a song and dance man from the British Music Hall. He knew as little about films as those producing them. No one ever wrote a script for the films. Everything was improvised on the spot. Chaplin's trademark hat and cane were merely an afterthought.

Chaplin was like everyone associated with the "gimmick." He didn't understand it. He was making $10,000 a week, yet he lived in the YMCA! He was on a train trip to New York when the train stopped in Amarillo, Texas. As he was shaving he looked out to see an entire town gathered at the station. To someone on the train he asked what all the people were doing there. He didn't realize they were there to see **him**.

Everyone knows how this story turned out. Hollywood became the mecca for glitz and glamour and Chaplin was a victim of the McCarthy mentality. The story about the emergence of Hollywood reminds us that luck can make a difference in the outcome of nearly everything we do. The early pioneering film makers didn't do too many things right but they were incredibly successful with those "stupid little movies." Today's reality is different. Organizations create their own luck, good or bad. Let's examine luck's two faces.

Face One

Weyerhauser is known as a timber producer that operates with bountiful timber resources. The company transforms trees into paper. The company is also involved in mortgage banking, garden products, home building, insurance, and pet supplies. In other words, they're a long way from their roots.

They aren't the only ones drifting from earth's core. Gerber Baby Foods diversified into toys, furniture, and trucking (yes, trucking). Campbell's soups stirred interest in salmon farming and meal delivery services. They even operate a chicken plant.

Back to Weyerhauser. The only kind of luck they've had lately is bad. Ditto for their 28,000 shareholders. Their paper mills are designed to process as much wood as they can. The end products are incidental to production levels. The mills that process the timber are inefficient and costly. The more lean competitors at Georgia-Pacific, Union Camp, and Louisiana-Pacific are making pulp fiction out of Weyerhauser.

Weyerhauser's ideas of how to operate a company were wrong. As a result they've had a series of setbacks (bad luck?). The setbacks started in 1986 with the elimination of the tax advantage for timber sales.

Changes are now underway to alter their fortunes. The strategic shifts in focus include restructuring how mill managers are rewarded, greater emphasis on paper products, and selling-off some of the businesses that aren't related to their core. These actions are intended to change their fate. Good luck!

Face Two

Luck's other face belongs to good. Some organizations seem to experience only good luck. The company that Soichiro Honda founded in 1948 is a classic example.

In 35 countries scattered around the globe, Honda prospers like few others. The company that produces cars, motorcycles, and power equipment has set a standard of excellence and success that is virtually unmatched.

In 1982, Honda became American industry's newest neighbor. It opened Honda of America Manufacturing (HAM). Its Marysville, Ohio plant was the first Japanese company to operate inside the United States.

This $24 billion giant offers a stark contrast to most American organizations. They have successfully used teamwork, quality, pride, continuous change, long-term relationships, effective marketing, respect for individuals, and production efficiency to become one of the world's "luckiest" companies. From a humble beginning of a $3,200 investment in 1948, Honda has created their own good luck through years of efficient and effective actions. They are a world leader at what they do. It is a position they aren't likely to lose soon.

Lights, Camera, Action

Lights, camera, action. In the movies, this sequence of events forms the structure of film-making. After the set is built, lighting is arranged. Lights are positioned at just the right angles to cast the precise glow on the performers. Lighting is used to amplify the mood and enhance the plot. Lighting is important but it's only one part of the trinity. After the lighting is set, in come the cameras.

The cameras are readied in strategic position to capture every important movement and facial expression. Angles are as important in camera work as they are in geometry and billiards. Cameras zoom in and out to highlight key sequences in the dialogue or help viewers feel the emotions displayed by the actors and actresses. Cameras help the viewer become one with the performer. Cameras are as indispensable as the lights.

Neither the lights nor the camera would have any lasting impact, however, if it wasn't for the **action**. Without action, all the preparation would have no meaning. The efforts of arranging the lighting and readying the cameras would be a wasted exercise. It is the linkage of these three separate activities that makes one important whole.

When the lights and camera come on, the action begins. Performers assume their roles and everyone on the sound stage or set works in unison to produce a product worthy of their collective efforts.

What is so **common** in film making is so often **ignored** by other organizations. After the organizational lights are arranged and the cameras readied, our directors take leave. They wait to see what someone else does, then they **react**.

Film making and television production are the best examples of what the Zeitgeist Manager is all about. You have to identify change and act! GM knew for almost a decade what it had to do. It watched as its competitors used different approaches to steal its proud history. When the hemorrhaging reached $15 million a day, GM finally applied a tourniquet. Bandage after bandage was applied. Will the mummy come back to life?

The history of management hasn't treated the **passive** manager with great respect. And up to now history has been **kind**.

In the future, successful organizations will depend on quick and aggressive action to be competitive and productive in the global village. Successful organizations in business, education, and government will take their cue from film's most famous sequence: Lights, camera, ACTION!

Vowels

Managing Back: Mugged by Reality is a book about **awareness**, **understanding**, and **action**. No matter what we know or how it is used, it all comes down to one important ingredient. The ability of organizations to succeed will always depend on **people**. Organizations are people. People are organizations. Organizations are the ultimate endorsement of the gestalt principle that the whole is greater than the sum of its parts.

How important are people to the success or failure of an organization? Many people give lip service to the importance. Some organizations, like Apple Computer, Inc. and Honda USA, have moved away from traditional approaches and operationalized the **power** of people. With them, people **really do** come first. Too many organizations however operate in **blissful ignorance** of human possibility.

Consider the English language. How important are the vowels *a, e, i, o,* and *u* to the transmission of information? These five symbols link the other 21 symbols into a recognizable and understandable form. Communication would be very different without them. So too with organizations and people. The following passage describes how important people are.

P pl r th l nk b tw n str ct r s, syst ms, sk lls, sh r d v l s, styl , nd st ff. P pl r th l nk t q l ty, nn v t n, c st m r s rv c , r p t t n, pr d cts, f n nc l s cc ss, nd rg n z t n l s rv v l. f m n y m k s the w rld g r nd, p pl m ke rg n z t ns g r nd.

Without the vowels, these symbols are meaningless. They are incoherent letters without any connection. If you found this short exercise difficult, consider what your organization would be like without people. It would be like words without vowels. In short, you wouldn't have an organization. Vowels and people have a lot in common. They are both indispensable.

If you want to know what it was that you couldn't read, read on.

People are the link between structures, systems, skills, shared values, style and staff. People are the link to quality, innovation, customer service, reputation, products, financial success, and organizational survival. If money makes the world go round, people make organizations go round.

Unnatural Law

It started simply enough. Someone found a way to bring humor to the trials and tribulations of everyday living. These gems of wisdom seem to capture life. They remind us that it really is better to laugh than cry.

One of the first expressions of frustration is known as Parkinson's Law. It states that any project can be expanded to accommodate all the time and money allocated to it. Not far behind Parkinson came the Peter Principle. Peter said that everyone rises to the level of their incompetence.

Parkinson and Peter didn't go far enough in describing frustration. Murphy's Law elevated it another notch. Murphy's Law is straightforward and simple. It says that everything that can go wrong will go wrong. Although no one seems to know who Murphy is, most people have experienced days that would make him proud.

Murphy's Law suggests that the universe is just a little perverse and no matter what is done, things don't work out as expected. It is possible that the expectations are flawed to begin with and therefore Murphy is entitled to be right.

A Bumper Crop

Murphy gets appropriate credit for his gem of wisdom but he may not get enough credit for the other important contribution he made. It was a take-off on Murphy's Law which started the bumper sticker craze. Part of the "enjoyment" of being stuck in traffic is learning more about our fellow human beings by what their bumper stickers say. There really isn't much difference between philosophy and a bumper sticker.

One of the first bumper stickers in memory describes Murphy as an optimist. It didn't stop there. The most recent message to grace our chrome billboards marks the final passing of the Victorian period. During this period of gentility, a long string of four-letter words became verboten.

Not anymore.

The newest version of Murphy's Law states that "(EXPLETIVE) HAPPENS." It is an irreverent, vulgar expression that emphatically makes the point. It's more extreme than Murphy's Law and conveys the message that things don't go right even when you do right.

The way most of our organizations are managed is **profoundly wrong**. In the 1990s we must arrive at a new standard of management practice. A standard where doing right improves the odds that things will go right. We can't afford expletives to happen. Organizations must become more competitive and more productive.

To avoid the expletives means a continuous search for Waldo. He will weave and dodge and attempt to hide, but successful management will depend on searching him out.

Waldo will continue to be the overlooked idea, the right choice, the correct approach, the plan not made, or the action not taken. He will continue to symbolize the correct structure and the effective process. Waldo is management's breakthrough thinking.

The new standard also means continuous focus on Zeitgeist. The essence of management changes and evolves. The very nature of management imposes a requirement of constant questioning, examination, and experimentation. The qualities essential to one particular period may be useless to another.

Consider the dramatic case of General Motors. In 1991 GM reached the lowest point in its history with a loss of $4.5 billion. The company announced a major restructuring that will claim 85,000 jobs and close 23 plants by the mid 1990s. The reason? To make the company lean and responsive.

The restless, mainstream automaker that once was the world leader is now ready to trade dominance for profitable market share. The strategies, structures, and systems which made them the king of the auto industry now leave them pawns.

Restructuring, lean, Six Sigma quality, customer service, innovation, risk, and empowerment are part of today's Zeitgeist. The message of Zeitgeist is to recognize **what** works today and **why.**

The message of *Managing Back: Mugged by Reality* is to focus, understand, and act.

First, we search for Waldo. Then, we learn the Zeitgeist lessons of our time. Finally, we use our tools applying the principles and ideas **pro actively**.

Waldo. Zeitgeist. Action.

For too long, we have been mugged by reality.

We **can** manage our way back!

Appendix

The Handcuff Puzzle

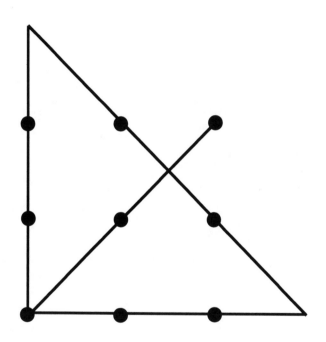

Bibliography

Abernathy, William J., and Hayes, Robert H. "Managing Our Way To Economic Decline." Harvard Business Review, July-August 1980, pp. 67-77.

Albrecht, Karl, and Zemke, Ron. Service America! New York: Warner Books, Inc., 1985.

Alfred, Richard L., and Weissman, Julie. Higher Education and the Public Trust: Improving Stature in Colleges and Universities. ASHE-ERIC Higher Education Report No. 6. Washington, D.C.: Association for the Study of Higher Education, 1987.

Alster, Norm. "A Third-Generation Galvin Moves Up." Forbes, April 30, 1990, pp. 57 - 62.

Andrews, Edmund L. "Breakdown Unnoticed For 6 Hours, AT&T Says." Austin American Statesman, September 19, 1991, p. A4.

Angel, Dan. Interview with Gene Stouder, Vice President & Director of Die Manufacturing-Microprocessor & Memory Technologies Group, Motorola, Austin, Texas, September 27, 1991.

Angel, Dan. Interview with Jerry Carlson, Vice President and General Manager, Entry Systems Division, Austin, Texas, October 9, 1991.

Auchincloss, Kenneth. "When Worlds Collide." Newsweek, Fall, Winter 1991, pp. 8-13.

"Audit Finds 25.7 Million Census Goofs." Austin American-Statesman, August 23, 1991, p. A4.

Avishai, Bernard, and Taylor, William. "Customers Drive a Technology-Driven Company: An Interview with George Fisher." Harvard Business Review, November-December 1989, pp. 107-114.

Bacon, Donald C. "How the Baldrige Winners Did It." Nation's Business, January 1989, pp. 32, 34.

Ballen, Kate. "Get Ready for Shopping at Work." Fortune, Feb.15, 1991, pp. 95, 98.

Barrett, William P. "The Best Little Hash House in Texas." Forbes, November 12, 1990, pp. 220-221.

Baumann, Marty. "Best and Worst P.O.'s." USA Today, November 5, 1991, p. 1E.

Belasco, James A. Teaching the Elephant to Dance: The Manager's Guide to Empowering Change. New York: Plume, 1991.

"Bell Cutbacks." USA Today, October 2, 1991, p. 1B.

Belton, Beth. "Jenny Craig Beefs Up Despite Market." USA Today, November 21, 1991, p. 3B.

Belluck, Pam. "Movie Blast to Recoup S&L Cash." Austin American-Statesman, January 8, 1992, p. A8.

Bernstein, Aaron. "How To Motivate Workers: Don't Watch 'Em." Business Week, April 29, 1991, p. 54.

Bernstein, Aaron. "Quality Is Becoming Job One in the Office, Too." Business Week, April 29, 1991, pp. 52-54.

Berss, Marcia. "Haircut Anyone?" Forbes, April 26, 1993, pp 128 & 129.

"Best Cars of the Year: Chrysler leads magazine lists." USA Today, Dec. 4, 1992, p.3D.

Biers, Dan. "After Battling Restrictions, Toys "R" Us Opens in Japan." Austin American-Statesman, December 20, 1991, p. D1, D4.

"Big Mac's Counter Attack." The Economist, Nov. 13, 1993, pp 71 & 72.

Blonston, Gary. "Government Jobs Grow Even During Hard Times." Austin American-Statesman, August 15, 1991, p. G1.

Bok, Derek. Universities and The Future. Durham, N.C.: Duke University Press, 1990.

Boyette, Joseph H., and Conn, Henry P. Workplace 2000: The Revolution Reshaping American Business. New York: Duton, 1991.

Brackey, Harriet Johnson. "McDonald's Growth May Be Stunted." USA Today, August 16, 1991, p. 3B.

Branco, Anthony, and Keller, John J. "The Sad Saga of Western Union's Decline." Business Week, December 14, 1987, pp. 108-114.

Bremner, Brian. "The Corporate Elite: Tough Times, Tough Bosses." Business Week, November 25, 1991, pp.174-179.

Breyer, R. Michelle. "GM To Phase Out 74,000 Jobs." Austin American-Statesman, December 19, 1991, pp. A1, A8.

Bridges, William. Managing Transitions: Making the Most of Change. Redding, Mass: Addison-Wesley, 1991.

Bryant, Web. "Long Line Of Job Cuts." USA Today, December 20, 1991, p. 1B.

Buffington, Perry W. "Capitalizing On Complaints." SKY, June 1991, pp. 33-38.

Button, Graham. "Another Loony Energy Subsidy." Forbes Magazine, December 9, 1991, p. 290.

Bylinsky, Gene. "Turning R&D Into Real Products." Fortune, July 2, 1990. pp. 72-77.

Byrne, John A. "In Retail, Bigger Can Be Better." Business Week, March 27, 1989, pp. 90, 92, 94.

Cain, Brad. "Oregon Launches Program To Abolish Traditional High School." Austin American-Statesman, July 25, 1991, p. C26.

"Campbell is Bubbling." Business Week, June 17, 1991, p 56

Calonius, Erik. "Federal Express's Battle Overseas." Fortune, Dec. 3, 1990, pp. 137-138, 140.

Caprino, Mariann. "Cost of Disasters: $4 Billion." Austin American-Statesman, December 18, 1991, p. D1.

Carey, John. "Top of the News: Food Labeling: The FDA Has The Right Ingredients."

Business Week, November 23, 1992, p. 42.

Carlson, Jerry M. "Technology Is Only Part Of The Solution To Education Problems." Austin American Statesman, September 17, 1991, p. A8.

Carnevale, Anthony P. America and the New Economy. Washington, D.C.: U.S. Department of Labor Employment and Training Administration, 1991.

Carroll, Doug. "Guest Gets Good Housekeeping." USA Today, Oct. 31, 1991, p. 11E.

Carroll, Doug. "Airlines Raise Grades." USA Today, November 12, 1991, p. 4B.

Carroll, Doug. "Hotels Trim Guest Perks, Gird For '90s." USA Today, Dec. 3, 1991, pp. 1-2B.

Carroll, Paul B. "IBM Is Likely In 1992 to Trim 20,000 Positions." The Wall Street Journal, November 20, 1991, pp. A1, A3.

Castro, Janice. "A Saucy Fight For A Slice Of The Pie." Time, April 18, 1988, p. 60.

Chakravarty, Subrata N. "We Have to Change the Playing Field." Forbes, February 4, 1991, pp. 82-86.

Chakravarty, Subrata N. "A Tale Of Two Companies" Forbes, May 27, 1991, pp. 86, 90, 92-94, 96.

Chira, Susan. "Report Card Shows U.S. Slow In Meeting Educational Goals." Austin American-Statesman, October 3, 1991, p. A21.

Chrysler Corporation. Information Package. Highland Park, Mich: Chrysler Corporation, 1992.

"Chrysler Surprises Street With $202 million Profit." Los Angeles Times, Oct. 21, 1992, p. 2D.

Cianci, Laura. "Business: Halliburton To Supervise Japanese Project." Dallas Times Herald, November 15, 1991, p. B3.

Cimmons, Marlene. "Federal Officials Spell Out Tougher Food Labeling Rules." Austin American-Statesman, November 7, 1991, pp. A1, A16.

"Classic Comeback For An Old Champ." U.S. News & World Report, July 22, 1985, p. 12.

Clements, Michael, and Healey, James R. "GM Names 7 More Plants For Closing." USA Today, December 4, 1992, p. B1.

Coddington, Ron. "USA Tops In Quality." USA Today, October 9, 1991, p. 1B.

"Consumers Can Make Banks Reduce Card Rates." USA Today, Nov. 6, 1991, p. 12A.

Cooper, James C., and Madigan, Kathleen. "Business Outlook: Nothing Ails America That A Few Million Jobs Couldn't Cure." Business Week, Nov. 23, 1992, p. 25.

Cox, James. "Coca-Cola Plans Salute To Its Biggest Flop." USA Today, April 19, 1990, p. 1B.

Craig, David. "Some Baldrige Winners Are Losers." USA Today, Oct. 10, 1991, p. 3B.

Craig, David. "Harley Stock Takes Turn For Worse." USA Today, Oct. 25, 1991, p. 3B.

Crosby, Philip B. Let's Talk Quality. New York: Plume, 1989.

"Crowned, Roger Maris." Time, September 16, 1991, p. 77.

Cutler, Laurel. "Consumers Are Tougher Customers." Fortune, July 3, 1989, p. 76.

Dart, Bob. "Nearly 35 Million Americans Lack Health Insurance, Report Says." Austin American-Statesman, December 12, 1991, p. A1.

Davenport, Carol. "America's Most Admired Corporations." Fortune, Jan. 30, 1989, pp. 68-94.

Davidow, William H. and Uttal, Bro. Total Customer Service: The Ultimate Weapon. New York: Harper & Row, 1989.

DeFao, Janine, "Study: U.S. Losing Market Share." Austin American-Statesman, November 14, 1991, p. H2.

DeMott, John S. "All Afizz Over the New Coke." Time, June 24, 1985, p. 60.

Dertouzos, Michael L., Lester, Richard K., and Solow, Robert M. Made in America: Regaining the Productive Edge. Cambridge, Mass.: MIT Press, 1990.

Desatnick, Robert L. "Service: A CEO's Perspective." Management Review, October 1987, pp. 41-45.

DeSimone, Bonnie. "Court Recorders," The Detroit News, Aug. 11, 1991, pp. 1B, 4B.

Deutsch, Claudia H. "How Is It Done? For a Small Fee..." New York Times, Oct. 27, 1991, p. F25.

DeVault, Mike. Interview with Richard D'Agostino, President, Personal Financial Assistant, Inc.(Charlotte, NC), Austin, Texas.

DeVault, Mike. Interview with Chris Bridenbaugh, Public Relations Director, Nordstrom (Seattle, Washington), Austin, Texas.

DeVault, Mike. Interview with Gordon Lambourne, Director of National Public Relations, Marriott Hotels (Resorts and Suites Division), Austin, Texas.

DeVault, Mike. Interview with Don Beaver, President, New Pig Corporation (Tipton, PA), Austin, Texas.

Donlon, Brian. "Fox First To Air Condom Ads." USA Today, November 13, 1991. A1.

"Douglas Layoffs." USA Today, December 5, 1991, 1B.

Dreyfuss, Joel. "Victories In The Quality Crusade." Fortune, Oct. 10, 1988, pp. 80-88.

Driscoll, Lisa. "Can Domino's Deliver?" Business Week, Oct. 28, 1991, pp. 136-140.

Dumaine, Brain. "How Managers Can Succeed Through Speed." Fortune, February 13, 1989, pp. 54-59.

Dumaine, Brian. "P&G Rewrites the Marketing Rules." Fortune, November 6, 1989, pp. 34-36, 38, 40, 42, 46, 48.

"Du Pont Layoffs." USA Today, October 2, 1991, p. 1B.

Dye, Lee. "Scientists Say They Can Correct Vision of Hubble During '93 Shuttle Flight." Austin American-Statesman, September 28, 1990, p. A2.

Eccles, Robert G. The Transfer Pricing Problem. Lexington, Mass.: Lexington Books, 1985.

Edwards, Roberta. Silly Fishermen. New York: Random House, 1989.

Einhorn, Cheryl. "One Word: Plastic." Barron's, Sept. 19, 1994, pps 29 - 33.

Ellis, James E. "H&R Block Expands Its Tax Base." Business Week, Apr. 22, 1991, p. 52.

Farley, Christopher John. "Virtual Reality Is Computer's Flying Carpet." USA Today, September 18, 1991, pp. 1-2D.

Fedor, Barnaby. "There's Still Plenty Of Room To Grow." New York Times, Jan. 9, 1994, p 5.

Fetterman, Mindy. "Soviets Court Fast-Track U.S. Firms." USA Today, October 2, 1991, p. 1A.

Fetterman, Mindy. "Autocratic Leaders Now Out Of Step." USA Today, December 9, 1991, pp. 1-2B.

Fetterman, Mindy, and Lawlor, Julia. "Workforce Redefined By Tough Times." USA Today, December 20, 1991, p. 1-2B.

Fetterman, Mindy, and Moore, Martha T. "Dueling Cereal Boxes." USA Today, October 29, 1991, 1B.

Fetterman, Mindy, and Wiseman, Paul. "Size Of Crisis Overwhelming Regulators." USA Today, June 12, 1991, p. 1-2A.

Fickenschir, Linda. "Master Card" New Chief Exec." American Banker. March 24, 1994 p. 15.

Fishbein, Ed. "Global Manufacturing: Cleaning Up." World Trade, November 1991, pp. 46,48,49.

Fisher, Anne B. "What Consumers Want In The 1990s." Fortune, January 29, 1990, pp. 108-112.

Fisk, Margaret Cronin. "White-Collar Boom." The National Law Journal, December 2, 1991, pp. 1.

Flint, Jerry. "The Game's Not Over." Forbes, April 30, 1990, pp. 76, 78,82.

Flint, Jerry. "The New Team's Plans For Moving Iron." Forbes, Oct. 1, 1990, pp. 76, 78, 82.

"Following Chrysler," The Economist, April 23, 1994, pp. 66 & 67.

Foust, Dean. "Why Giant Foods Is A Gargantuan Success," Business Week, December 4, 1989, p. 80.

Foust, Dean, and others. "How Deep Is The Hole." Business Week, Dec. 9, 1991, pp. 30-32.

Frantz, Douglas, and Bates, James. "Three BCCI Figures Charged With Fraud." Austin American-Statesman, November 16, 1991, p. C5.

"Fuji To Use Kodak CD Technology." USA Today, September 19, 1991, p. 2B.

Galloway, Paul. "Blondie Goes To Work." Austin American-Statesman, August 29, 1991, pp. D1, D6.

Gannes, Stuart. "America's Fastest-Growing Companies." Fortune, May 23, 1988, pp. 28, 30-32, 36, 40.

German, Eric, and others. "Coke Tampers With Success." Newsweek, May 6, 1985, pp. 50-52.

Gerrow, Thomas. "Technology Sets New Tone for Automotive Paints," Austin American-Statesman, October 3, 1991, pp. C1, C5.

Gerrow, Thomas. "Customer Service Wins Buyer Loyalty." Austin American-Statesman, November 7, 1991, pp. C1, C4.

Gibbs, Nancy. "How America Has Run Out of Time." Time, Apr. 24, 1989, pp. 58 - 67.

Gill, Mark Stuart. "Stalking Six Sigma." Business Month, January 1990, pp. 42-46.

Goodman, Ellen. "What Blondie Will Learn About the Working World." Austin American-Statesman, September 10, 1991, p. A9.

Goodman, Adam. "ESCO...On Its Own: Spinoff Hit With Losses in 1st Year." St. Louis Post-Dispatch, November 10, 1991, pp. 1E, 8E.

Goodman, Adam. "McDonnell Pins Its Commercial Hopes On Asia." St. Louis Post Dispatch, November 24, 1991, pp. 1E, 3E.

Grassmuck, Karen. "Throughout the 80's, Colleges Hired More Non-Teaching Staff Than Other Employees." The Chronicle of Higher Education, August 14, 1991, pp. A22-23.

Gross, Neil. "Taking On Japan: Why U.S. Business Wants Backup." Business Week, November 13, 1989, p. 111.

Grun, Bernard. The Timetables of History. New York: Simon and Schuster, 1982.

Guenther, Robert. "Citicorp Offers Mortgage Commitments In 15 Minutes." The Wall Street Journal, February 8, 1989, p. B1.

Hammonds, Keith H. "Corning's Class Act." Business Week, May 13, 1991, pp. 68-76.

Hansell, Saul. "At Visa, New Quest For Growth." New York Times, Oct. 7, 1993, page D1.

Hansell, Saul. "The New Deal At American Express." New York Times. July 31, 1994, pp 1 - 6.

Hartman, Curtis. "The Best-Managed Franchises in America." INC., October 1989, pp. 68-70, 74-75.

Hasson, Judy. "Staggering Rise In Uninsured." USA Today, Dec. 15, 1993, p 4A

Hawkins, Stacy L. "'Lot More to Advanced TV Than Just Sharper Picture'," USA Today, August 12, 1991, p. 9A.

Hawkins, Stacy L. "High-Definition TV On Horizon," USA Today, Aug. 12, 1991, p. 9A.

Hayes, Robert H. "Strategic Planning-Forward In Reverse?" Harvard Business Review, November-December 1985, pp. 111-119.

Hayes, Robert H., and Jaikumar, Ramchandran. "Manufacturing's Crisis: New Technology..." Harvard Business Review, September/October 1988, pp. 77-83.

Hayner, Anne M. "Apple Power." Manufacturing Engineering, July 1989, p. 38.

Hays, Thomas C. "Behind Wal-Mart's Surge, A Web Of Suppliers." The New York Times, July 1, 1991, pp. D1-2.

Hector, Gary. "It's Banquet Time For BankAmerica." Fortune, June 3, 1991, pp. 69-73.

Hellmich, Nancy. "Big Changes Proposed For Food Labels." USA Today, November 6, 1991, p. 1-2D.

Hendley, Vicky. "Education Leader Urges Colleges Not To Sacrifice Technology," The Times, March 12, 1991, p. 7.

Henkoff, Ronald. "What Motorola Learns From Japan." Fortune, April 24, 1989, pp. 157, 160, 164, 168.

Henkoff, Ronald. "Keeping Motorola On A Roll." Fortune, April 18, 1994, pp 67 - 78.

Heskett, James L., Sasser, Jr., W. Earl, and Hart, Chistopher. Service Breakthroughs: Changing the Rules Of The Game. New York: Free Press, 1990.

"Hey America, Coke Are It!" Newsweek, July 22, 1985, p. 40.

Higher Education & National Affairs. "Debate Focuses on Quality of Higher Ed," American Council on Education, May 1991, p. 5.

Hillkirk, John, and Jacobson, Gary. Grit, Guts & Genius: True Tales of Mega Success. Boston: Houghton Mifflin Company, 1990.

"Hubble Telescope Suffers New Glitch." Austin American-Statesman, Sept. 4, 1991, p. A8.

Huey, John. "Wal-Mart Will It Take Over the World?" Fortune, January 30, 1989, pp. 52-56, 58, 61.

Huey, John. "America's Most Successful Merchant." Fortune, September 23, 1991, pp. 46-48, 50, 54, 58-59.

Hume, Scott. "McDonald's." Advertising Age, January 29, 1991, p. 32.

Hyatt, Joshua. "Betting The Farm." Inc., December 1991, pp. 36-48.

"IBM Mulls Reorganization." Austin American-Statesman, Nov. 19, 1991, pp. C7-8.

Isenberg, Daniel J. "The Tactics of Strategic Opportunism." Harvard Business Review, March-April 1987, pp. 92-97.

Johnson, Kevin. "Tylenol Liability Trial Begins," USA Today, May 13, 1991, p. 3A.

Johnson, Robert. "Fast-Food Chains Draw Criticism for Marketing Fare as Nutritional." Wall Street Journal, April 6, 1987, p. 27 (W); p. 31 (E).

Johnson, Robert. "McDonald's Combines Dead Man's Advice with Lively Strategy." Wall Street Journal, December 18, 1987, pp. 1, 12.

Kadlec, Daniel, and Cauley, Leslie. "IBM To Cut 25,000 More Jobs, Spending: Layoff

Policy, Divident May Be Affected." USA Today, December 16, 1992, p. B1.

Kalette, Denise. "IRS Will Test Touch-tone Phone Filing," USA Today, Oct. 1, 1991, page 1H.

Kearns, David T., and Doyle, Denis P. Winning the Brain Race. New York: Kaupman & Company, 1988.

Kearns, David T. "Quality In Copiers, Computers, And Floor Cleaning." Management Review, February 1989, pp. 61-63.

Kerwin, Kathleen. "Top Of The News: Mr. S & L Faces The Music." Business Week, November 25, 1991, p. 36.

"Kids' Inventions Merit Attention," USA Today, June 27, 1991, p. 6D.

Kim, James. "Xerox Moves To Duplicate Success." USA Today, Dec. 4, 1991, p. 3B.

Kindel, Stephen. "Sweet Chariots." Financial World, Jan. 18, 1994, pp 47-54.

Kimball, Allan C. "Homebuyers Hit For Billions Extra," Austin Business Journal, September 2, 1991, p. 1, 6.

Kimball, Allan C. "Sager: Supercuts Success Story." Austin Business Journal, October 14, 20, 1991, pp. 5-6.

Kimberly, John R., and Quinn, Robert E. Managing Organizational Transitions. Homewood, Ill: Dow-Jones-Irwin, 1984.

Kirkpatrick, John. "Quality Rewarded." Dallas Morning News, Oct. 19, 1994, pp 1-2D.

Kleege, Stephen. "Visa Bars It's Commercial - Card Issuers." American Banker, October 22, 1993, p 15.

Kleege, Stephen. "Master Card Strategist." American Banker, Jan. 12, 1994, p 13.

Knepper, Mike. "New Life For A Pipe Dream," American Way, Nov. 15, 1991, pp. 30-32.

Knowlton, Christopher. "How Disney Keeps The Magic Going." Fortune, December 4,

1989, pp. 111-112, 114, 116, 120, 124, 128, 132.

Knudson, Mary. "Medicare Supplier Rules Tightened." Austin American-Statesman, November 2, 1991, p. A26.

Koepp, Stephen. "Pul-eeze! Will Somebody Help Me?" Time, Feb. 2, 1987, pp. 48-55.

Koselka, Rita. "Mickey's Midlife Crisis." Forbes, May 13, 1991, pp. 42-43.

Kowalski, Tom. "Sanders Goes Back to Lions $4.2M Richer." USA Today, Aug. 13, 1991, p. 1C.

Krolicki, Kevin. "Akers Targets 20,000 Job Cuts For IBM In 1992." Austin American-Statesman, November 8, 1991, p. B1.

Ladendorf, Kirk. "State-of-the-Art Laundries," Austin American-Statesman, August 28, 1991, pp. B5-6.

Ladendorf, Kirk. "MCC Wins Patent For Breakthrough," Austin American-Statesman, October 5, 1991, p. E1.

Laird, Bob. "Breaking The Speed Barrier." USA Today, September 13, 1991, p. 1C.

Land, Mark. "Money: IBM Is Said To Sell Chips To Hyundai." USA Today, Oct. 9, 1991, p. 1B.

Land, Mark. "Bonus Section: IBM Introduces Its First Personal Computer In..." USA Today, October 21, 1991, p. 1E.

Land, Mark. "Time Line: A Quick History of the Personal Computer." USA Today, October 21, 1991, p. 1B.

Land, Mark. "On Warpath Against Taped Phone Pitches." USA Today, Nov. 8, 1991, p. 4B.

Lawlor, Julia. "A Million People Quit Job Search." USA Today, Nov. 21, 1991, pp. 1-2B.

LeBoeuf, Michael. How to Win Customers and Keep Them for Life. New York: Berley Books, 1987.

Leerhsen, Charles. "How Disney Does It." Newsweek, April 3, 1989, pp. 48-54.

Leinberger, Paul, and Tucker, Bruce. The New Individualists: The Generation After The Organization Man. New York: Harper Collins, 1991.

Lempert, Philip. "More Choices For A Choosier You." Parade Magazine, Nov. 10, 1991, pp. 8-9.

Light, Larry, and Farrell, Christopher. "Are You Really Insured?" Business Week, August 5, 1991, pp. 42-48.

Little, Rod. "Deposit Protection." USA Today, September 10, 1991, p. 1B.

Little, Rod, "USA Snapshots: Drugs Cost More In USA." USA Today, Sept. 25, 1991, p. A1.

Loden, Marilyn, and Rosener, Judy B. Workforce America! Managing Employee

Diversity As A Vital Resource. Homewood, Ill: Business One Irwin, 1991.

Longo, Don. "Meeting The Wal-Mart Way." Discount Store News. Jan. 20, 1994, p 15.

Loomis, Carol J. "Naked Came The Insurance Buyer." Fortune, June 10, 1985, pp. 68-72.

McCann, Bill. "Reorganized 7-Elevens Test Changes In Austin." Austin Business Journal, October 14-20, 1991, p. 3.

McLean-Ibrahim, Elys. "USA Snapshots: Satellite Score." USA Today, Sept. 13, 1991, p. 1A.

Main, Jeremy. "Detroit's Cars Really Are Getting Better." Fortune, Feb. 2, 1987, pp. 90-98.

Main, Jeremy. "The Winning Organization." Fortune, Sept. 26, 1988, pp. 50-52, 56, 60.

"The Managers Best." Business Week, January 14, 1991, pp. 130-131.

Maney, Kevin. "Taste Testing Includes BK`s Olive Burger." USA Today, Aug. 16, 1991, pp. 1-2A.

Maney, Kevin. "Coke Recognizes Republics." USA Today, August 30, 1991, p. 2B.

Maney, Kevin, and Lawlor, Julia. "Companies Shifting To Thinner Ranks." USA Today, August 6, 1991, pp. 1-2A.

Manor, Robert. "Chrysler Smoothing The Way For New Minivan." St. Louis Post-Dispatch, November 17, 1991, pp. 1A, 9A.

Markoff, John. "IBM To Set Up Separate Units." Austin American-Statesman, December 6, 1991, pp. C1, C10.

Martowe, Gene. "European Markets Lure Manufacturers." Tampa Tribune, December 22, 1991, Business and Finance p. 1.

Martz, Larry, and Clift, Eleanor. "Who Says There's No Free Lunch?" Newsweek, October 14, 1991, pp. 30-31.

Maynard, Micheline. "Iacocca Looks Down Road for Chrysler." USA Today, Oct. 17, 1991, p. 6B.

Maynard, Micheline. "GM May Cut 11,000 More Jobs." USA Today, Nov. 13, 1992, p. A1.

Maynard, Micheline. "Profitable, 'Lean' Firm Is The Goal." USA Today, Dec. 19, 1991, p. 1.

"McDonald's Test is Child's Play." USA Today, Aug. 30, 1991, p. 7B.

Memmott, Mark. "Layoffs Mount As Firms Look For Profits." USA Today, Oct. 4, 1991, pp. 1-2B.

Memmott, Mark. "Experts: Recession Pains Will Bring Gains." USA Today, Dec. 20, 1991, p. 1B.

Mescon, Michael H. and Mescon, Timothy S. "On Management: Structuring Survival." SKY, Aug. 1991, pp. 86, 88, 89.

Miller, Eric (ed.). Future Vision. Illinois: Research Alert, 1991.

Miller, Nancy. "Salomon Executives' Bonuses Trimmed 20%." USA Today, Dec. 9, 1991, p. 1B.

Mintzberg, Henry. "Crafting Strategy." Harvard Business Review, July-August 1987, pp. 66-75.

Minzesheimer, Bob. "Oops! House Members Bounce 4,325 Checks," USA Today, September 20, 1991, p. 1A.

Mitchell, Russell. "Masters of Innovation: How 3M Keeps Its New Products Coming." Business Week, April 10, 1989, pp. 58-63.

"Money: Christmas-bonus Cuts To Save GM $60 Million." USA Today, Nov. 29, 1991, p. 1B.

"Money: RTC to Auction $100M Of Loans." USA Today, December 4, 1991, pp 7B.

Monninger, Joseph. "Fast Food." American Heritage, April 1988, pp. 68-75.

Monopoly®. "Monopoly® Game Fact Sheet." Parker Brothers, Beverly, MA.

Montague, Bill. "Insurance Firm Turns Away Hundreds." USA Today, July 16, 1991, pp. 1-2A.

Montague, Bill. "Insurance Rating Firms Draw Fire." USA Today, July 22, 1991, p. 1B.

Montague, Bill. "Critics Say Agencies Failed During Crisis." USA Today, Aug. 6, 1991, p. 6B.

Montague, Bill. "The Public Is Fed Up With High Rates." USA Today, November 4, 1991, pp. 1-2A.

Montague, Bill. "Plastic Becomes Politically Charged Issue." USA Today, November 20, 1991, p. 1B.

Montague, Bill. "A.M. Best Upgrades Rating System." USA Today, Jan. 14, 1992, p. 4B.

Moore, Jonathan. "Texas Congressman Drive On Taxpayers' Tab While At Home." Austin American-Statesman, November 22, 1991, p. B3.

Morgenson, Gretchen. "Power Shift." Forbes, November 11, 1991, pp. 38-39.

Morrow, David J. "Iacocca Talks On What Ails Detroit." Fortune, Feb. 12, 1990, pp. 68, 69, 72.

Moser, Penny. "The McDonald's Mystique." Fortune, July 4, 1988, pp. 112-115.

Naisbitt, John, and Aburdene, Patricia. Re-inventing the Corporation: Transforming your job and your company for the new information society. New York: Warner Books, 1985.

National Center on Education and the Economy. America's Choice: High Skills or Low Wages! Rochester, NY: National Center on Education and the Economy, 1990.

Neuborne, Ellen. "Low Fat, To Go." USA Today, July 31, 1991, p. 1B.

Neuborne, Ellen. "Hungry? No Cash? Try McVisa." USA Today, Sept. 17, 1991, p. 6B.

Neuborne, Ellen. "Color Crayola Blush Red." USA Today, September 27, 1991, p. 1B.

Neuborne, Ellen. "Home Depot Nails Down Success." USA Today, Jan. 14, 1992, p. 3B.

Nordstrom. Annual Report 1990, Nordstrom, Inc. and Subsidiaries, Seattle, WA.

Novaha, Skujiro. "Toward Middle-Up-Down Management: Accelerating Information Creation." Sloan Management Review. 1988, 29 (1), pp. 9-18.

Nulty, Peter. "The Soul of an Old Machine." Fortune, May 21, 1990, pp. 67-72.

Office of Planning, Budget and Evaluation, Tough Choices. Washington, D.C.: U.S. Department of Education, 1991.

Ono, Yumiko. "Marketplace: Ads For Vitamin Drinks Pack American Punch." The Wall Street Journal, November 20, 1991, p. B1.

Orsburn, Jack D., and others. Self-Directed Work Teams: The New American Challenge. Illinois: Business One Irwin, 1990.

Osborn, Michelle. "The Wharton School." USA Today, October 2, 1991, pp. 1-3B.

Osborn, Michelle. "Number of Women In Workforce Levels Off." USA Today, October 24, 1991, p. 2B.

Osborne, David, and Gaebler, Ted. Reinventing Government. New York: Addison-Wesley, 1992.

Ozanian, Michael. "Mouse Trap." Financial World. March 15, 1994, pp 28 - 30.

Paltrow, Scot J. "Allied Cuts 5,000 Jobs in Large Restructuring." Austin American-Statesman, October 10, 1991, p. B4.

Papiornik, Richard. "Mac Attack?" Financial World, April 12, 1994, pp 28-30.

Par'e, Terence P. "Banks Discover the Consumer." Fortune, Feb. 12, 1990, pp. 96-97, 100, 104.

Pascale, Richard Tanner. Managing on the Edge: How the Smartest Companies Use Conflict to Stay Ahead. New York: Simon and Schuster, 1990.

Pennar, Karen. "America's Quest Can't Be Half-Hearted." Business Week, June 8, 1987, p. 136.

Persinos, John F. "Going Bare." Inc., October 1985, pp. 72-84.

Peters, Tom. Thriving on Chaos. New York: Harper & Row, 1988.

Peters, Tom. "Businesses Can Clean Up By Going Clean And Green." Austin American-Statesman, November 3, 1991, p. H3.

Petersen, Donald E., and Hillkirk, John. A Better Idea: Redefining the Way Americans Work. Boston: Houghton Mifflin, 1991.

Petersen, Donald E., and Hillkirk, John. "Petersen's Better Idea: Retired CEO Tells Bosses to Listen Up." USA Today, September 20, 1991, pp. 1-2A.

Peterson, Thane, Zellner, Wendy, and Woodruff, David. "All That Lean Isn't Turning Into Green." Business Week, November 18, 1991, pp. 39-40.

Phillips, Michael Max. "Senators Vow to Change Laws Governing Credit Reporters." Austin American-Statesman, October 23, 1991, p. D2.

"Pile 'em High And Go Bust." The Economist, July 7, 1990, p.60.

Pogoda, Dianne, "Expansion Plans At Wal-Mart." Men's Wear Daily. Sept. 16, 1994, p 17.

Pomice, Eva, and Cohen, Warren. "Business: The Toughest Companies In America." U.S. News & World Report, October 28, 1991, pp. 65-66, 68, 73, 74.

"Postal Service To Trim 47,000 Jobs By 1995." Austin American-Statesman, Sept. 27, 1991, p. A18.

Poole, Claire. "Shirt Sleeves To Shirt Sleeves." Forbes, March 4, 1991, pp. 52-56.

Quickel, Stephen W. "Management Joins the Computer Age." Business Month, May 1989, pp. 42, 44-46.

Ramirez, Anthony. "Low-Fat McDonald's Burger Is Planned To Answer Critics." The New York Times, March 13, 1991, pp. A1, D9.

Rebello, Kathy. "Sculley Banks On Software Innovation." USA Today, Aug. 2, 1991, p. 1B.

Reed, J.D. "Rattling The Chains." Time, October 23, 1991, pp. 95, 99.

"Refund Enclosed For Passive Restraint Systems." State Farm Insurance Companies, Bulk Mailing, November 1991.

Reich, Robert B. "Entrepreneurship Reconsidered: The Team As Hero." Harvard Business Review, May-June 1987, pp. 77-83.

Reid, Peter C. Well Made in America: Lessons from Harley-Davidson on Being the Best. New York: McGraw-Hill, 1990.

"Retailing's Golden Rules." U.S. News & World Report, March 12, 1990, p. 19.

Rice, Faye, and others. "Leaders Of The Most Admired." Fortune, January 29, 1990, Vol. 121, pp. 40-43, 46. 50, 54.

Richter, Paul. "Report: U.S. Schools Back At '70s Levels." Austin American-Statesman, October 1, 1991, pp. A2.

Rosato, Donna. "Wireless PC Gives Users An Office To Go." USA Today, Aug. 14, 1991, p. 1A.

Rosato, Donna. "Home Software: Flying Better." USA Today, Sept. 13, 1991, p. 1B.

Rosato, Donna. "Moneyline: Saturn To Bag It." USA Today, Nov. 21, 1991, p. 1B.

Rosato, Donna. "Moneyline: Brewing Drinks." USA Today, Dec. 4, 1991, p. B1.

Rosenbaum, David E. "Members of Congress Seen As Corrupt, Survey Reports." Austin American-Statesman, October 10, 1991, p. A3.

Rothenberg, Al. "Chrysler: Moving Too Fast?". Ward's Auto World, Aug. 1994, pp. 34 & 35.

Rothman, Andrea. "The Racy Viper Is Already A Winner For Chrysler." Business Week, November 4, 1991, pp. 36-38.

Rudnitsky, Howard. "An Excess of Plastic." Forbes, February 4, 1991, pp. 52, 56.

"Runaway Train Rolls 40 Miles Without Crew." Austin American-Statesman, November 7, 1991, p. A. 21.

Samuelson, Robert J. "The Boss as Welfare Cheat." Newsweek, Nov. 11, 1991, p. 55.

Saporito, Bill. "The Fix Is In At Home Depot." Fortune, Feb. 29, 1988, pp. 74-75, 79.

Saporito, Bill. "Companies That Compete Best." Fortune, May 22, 1989, pp. 36-44.

Saporito, Bill. "Competition: Can Anyone Win The Coffee War." Fortune, May 21, 1990, pp. 97, 100.

Saporito, Bill. "Money & Markets: Who's Winning The Credit Card War." Fortune, July 2, 1990, pp. 66-70.

Saporito, Bill. "Is Wal-Mart Unstoppable?" Fortune, May 6, 1991, pp. 50, 52, 54, 58-59.

Saporito, Bill. "Melting Point In The Plastic War." Fortune, May 20, 1991, pp.71-72, 76-77.

Saporito, Bill. "Campbell Soup Gets Piping Hot." Fortune, Sept. 9, 1991, pp. 142-148.

Saporito, Bill. "The Toppling of King James." Fortune, Jan. 11, 1993, pp 42 & 43.

Sawaya, Zina. "Focus Through Decentralization." Forbes, Nov. 11, 1991, pp. 242, 244.

Schlender, Brenton R. "How Levi Strauss Did An LBO Right." Fortune, May 7, 1990, pp. 105-107.

Schnaars, Steven P. Megamistakes. New York: The Free Press, 1989.

Schneidawind, John. "Technology Frees Many From Pain." USA Today, June 17, 1991, pp. 1B-2B.

Schneidawind, John, and Land, Mark. "Customers Demand An Explanation." USA Today, September 19, 1991, pp. 1-2B.

Schneidawind, John. "AT&T Plans to Stop Billing Ex-Customers." USA Today, October 30, 1991, p. 1B.

Schroeder, Michael. "The Recasting of Alcoa." Business Week, Sept. 9, 1991, pp. 62-64.

Schiller, Zachary, Zellner, Wendy, and Stodghill II, Ron. "Clout: How Giant Retailers Are Revolutionizing the Way Consumer Products Are Bought and Sold." Business Week, December 21, 1992, pp. 66-73.

Seidman, L. William, and Skancke, Steven L. Productivity: The Proven Path to Excellence In U.S. Companies. New York: Simon & Schuster, 1990.

Sellers, Patricia. "Why Bigger Is Badder at Sears." Fortune, Dec. 5, 1988, pp. 79-82, 84.

Sellers, Patricia. "Selling: Coke Gets Off Its Can In Europe." Fortune, August 13, 1990, pp. 68-70, 72, 73.

Sensenbrenner, Joseph. "Quality for Cities." Nation's Business, Oct. 1991, pp. 60, 62.

Sharn, Lori. "Wind-shear Systems Now Up At 110 Airports," USA Today, Oct. 24, 1991, p. 7A.

Sheets, Kenneth R. "How Wal-Mart Hits Main St." U.S. News & World Report, March 13, 1989, pp. 53-55.

Shook, Robert L. Honda: An American Success Story. New York: Prentice Hall Press, 1988.

"Shrinking Banks." USA Today, October 2, 1991, p. B1.

Sia, Richard H.P. "Auditors Say Senators' Meal Tabs Overdue." Austin American-Statesman, October 4, 1991, p. A6.

Sims, Calbin. "Walt Disney Reinventing Itself." New York Times, April 28, 1994, p 1.

Skidmore, David. "Bailout's End Remains Elusive." Austin American-Statesman, September 19, 1991, p. 1F.

Sherman, Stratford P. "How Philip Morris Diversified Right." Fortune, Oct. 23, 1989, pp. 120-128.

Smith, Emily T. "Doing It For Mother Earth." Business Week, Jan. 15, 1992, pp. 44, 46, 49.

Sontag, Sherry. "Business Watch: Investors Use Clout In the Corporate Governance Battle." The National Law Journal, December 2, 1991, pp. 23, 31-32.

Spencer, Leslie, Bollwerk, Jan, and Morais, Richard C. "The Not So Peaceful World of Greenpeace." Forbes, November 11, 1991, pp.174-180.

Sprout, Alison L. "America's Most Admired Corporations." Fortune, February 11, 1991, pp. 52-54, 57, 60-63, 69-70, 74-76, 78-79.

Staimer, Marcia. " USA Snapshots: Leading U.S. Prescription Drugs." USA Today, September 23, 1991, p. D1.

Star, Marlene. "TIAA - CREF Looks To Boost Returns." Pensions & Investments. Nov. 1, 1993, p 31.

Steffy, Loren. "Business: Top Firms Expecting To Move On." Dallas Times Herald, November 15, 1991, p. B1.

Stevens, Mark. "Turnaround Tricks: Getting A Company Back On Its Feet." Working Woman, December 1990, pp. 45-46, 48.

Stewart, Sally Ann. "Keating Guilty In Lincoln S&L Fraud Case." USA Today, Dec. 5, 1991, p. 1B.

Stewart, Thomas A. "The New American Century." Fortune, 1991, pp. 12-23.

Streufert, Siegfried, and Swezey, Robert W. Complexity, Managers, and Organizations. Orlando, Fla.: Academic Press, 1986.

Taylor, Alex III. "Autos: The New Drive to Revive GM." Fortune, April 9, 1990, pp. 52-57, 60, 61.

Taylor, Alex III. "Can Iacocca Fix Chrysler—Again?" Fortune, Apr. 8, 1991, pp. 50-54.

Taylor, Frederick W. Principles of Scientific Management. New York: W.W. Norton & Company, 1911.

"Texas Instruments To Lay Off 240 Workers, Including 30 In Austin." Austin American-Statesman, October 23, 1991, p. B4.

"The Comeback Kid." The Economist, Oct. 2, 1993, pp 88 & 89.

"The Managers Best." Business Week, January 14, 1991, pp 130-131

The New York Public Library Desk Reference. New York: Stonesong Press, 1989.

The Secretary's Commission on Achieving Necessary Skills, U.S. Department of Labor. What Work Requires of Schools: A SCANS Report for America 2000. Washington, D.C.: U.S. Department of Labor, 1991.

Therrien, Lois. "The Rival Japan Respects." Business Week, Nov. 13, 1989, pp. 108-110, 114.

Therrien, Lois. "McRisky." Business Week, October 21, 1991, pp. 114-117, 120, 122.

Therrien, Lois. "The Man Who's Shaking The Golden Arches." Business Week, October 21, 1991, p. 117.

Therrien, Lois. "The Upstarts Teaching McDonald's A Thing Or Two." Business Week, October 21, 1991, p. 122.

3M, Our Story So Far: Notes from the first 75 years of 3M Company. St. Paul, Minn.: 3M, 1977.

"TIAA - CREF Turns 75." Institutional Investor, Oct., 1993, p 220.

Ticer, Scott, and others. "Why Zapmail Finally Got Zapped." Business Week, October 13, 1986, pp. 48-49.

Toffler, Alvin. Future Shock. New York: Bantom Books, 1971.

Toffler, Alvin. Power Shift: Knowledge, Wealth, and Violence at the Edge of the 21st Century. New York: Bantam, 1990.

Tomasko, Robert M. Downsizing. New York: American Management Association, 1990.

Treece, James, B., and Zellner, Wendy. "The Flashing Signal at Chrysler: Danger Dead

Ahead." Business Week, June 18, 1990, pp. 44, 46.

Treece, James B., and Woodruff, David. "Crunch Time Again for Chrysler." Business Week, March 25, 1991, pp. 92-94.

Trump, Donald J., and Schwartz, Tony. Trump: The Art of the Deal. New York: Warner Books, 1987.

Tucker, William. "More Money." Forbes, December 9, 1991, p. 184.

Tushman, Michael, and Nadler, David. "Organizing for Innovation." California Management Review, 1986, XXVII (3), pp. 74-75.

"2 Washington Memorials Scheduled for Face Lifts." Austin American-Statesman, December 19, 1991, p. A7.

United States General Accounting Office. "Resolution Trust Corporation: Update on Funding and Performance." United States General Accounting Office, June 11, 1991.

Usdansky, Margaret L. "Numbers Game, USA Style." USA Today, Oct. 25, 1991, pp. A1, A8.

Uttal, Bro. "Companies That Serve You Best." Fortune, Dec 7, 1987, pp. 98-101, 104, 108.

Verity, John W. "Information Processing: A Slimmer IBM May Still Be Overweight." Business Week, December 18, 1989, pp.107, 108.

Verity, John W. "Special Report: Deconstructing the Computer Industry." Business Week, November 23, 1992, pp: 90-100.

Vigoda, Arlene. "Low-fat' Fare Is Plentiful, But Not All It Seems." USA Today, August 16, 1991, p. 4D.

Waggoner, John. "The $113.9 Billion _Oops'," USA Today, July 18, 1991, p. 1A.

Waggoner, John. "Jobless Report Slams Rates." USA Today, Dec. 20, 1991, p. 1B.

Waggoner, John. "Baldrige Winners Honored." USA Today, December 15, 1992, p. B1.

"Wal-Mart Stores Penny Wise." Business Month, December 1988, p. 42.

Walsh, Michael. "Tough Times, Tough Bosses." Business Week, Nov. 25, 1991, pp. 174-179.

Walton, Mary. The Deming Management Method. New York: Putnam Publishing Group. 1986.

Ward, Bernie. "Hiring Out." Sky, August 1991, pp. 37-45.

Ward, Sam. "Cutting Back." USA Today, August 29, 1991, p. 1B.

Wartzman, Rick. "McDonnell Douglas In Preliminary Pact To Sell Jetliner Stake To Taiwanese Firm." The Wall Street Journal, November 20, 1991, pp. A3.

Waterman, Jr. Robert H. The Renewal Factor: How the Best Get and Keep the Competitive Edge. New York: Bantam Books, 1987.

Watkins, Beverly T. "Using Computers to Teach Basic Skills," The Chronicle of Higher Education, October 2, 1991, pp. A23-24, 26.

Watkins, Beverly T. "Test Questions Stockpiled and Exams Created and Scored by Computer System at Miami-Dade Medical Campus," The Chronicle of Higher Education, October 16, 1991, p. 25, 39.

Watterson, Bill. The Essential Calvin And Hobbes: A Calvin and Hobbes Treasury. Kansas City, Mo.: Universal Press, 1988.

Weber, J. "Campbell is Bubbling." Business Week, June 17, 1991, pp. 56-57.

Weber, Joseph. "Special Report: When Benefits—And Jobs—Are Deconstructed." Business Week, November 23, 1992, p. 100.

Weiner, Steve. "Golf Balls, Motor Oil and Tomatoes." Forbes, Oct. 30, 1989, pp. 130-131, 134.

Weiner, Steve. "Retailing." Forbes, January 8, 1990, pp. 192, 194, 196, 198.

Weiner, Steve. "It's Not Over Until It's Over." Forbes, May 28, 1990, pp, 58-64.

Weiner, Steve. "Staying On Top In A Tough Business." Forbes, May 27, 1991, pp. 46-48.

"What's News: World-Wide: The Senate Ethics Committee Voted." The Wall Street Journal, November 20,1991, p. A1.

"Why is Sky Falling on Mutual Benefit?" USA Today, July 17, 1991, p. 4B.

Wiggenhorn, William. "Motorola U: When Training Becomes an Education." Harvard Business Review, July-August 1990, pp. 71-83.

Wilcox, Gregory J. "Bookstop Battles Crown For Superstore Dominance In L.A." Austin American-Statesman, December 8, 1991, pp. H1, H10.

"Will Things Still Go Better With Coke?" U.S. News & World Report, May 6, 1985, p. 14.

Wilson, David L. "Technology Update," The Chronicle of Higher Education, September 4, 1991, p. A33.

Wiseman, Paul. "USA Losing Its Edge In Technology," USA Today, Mar. 21, 1991, p. 1B.

Witt, Louise. "Business Watch: FDIC Criticizes Firms' Costs In BNE Failure." The National Law Journal, December 2, 1991, pp. 23.

Wloszczyna, Susan. "Who's Martin Handford?" USA Today, Sept. 10, 1991, p. 1D.

Womack, James P., Jones, Daniel T., and Roos, Daniel. The Machine That Changed The World. New York: Macmillan, 1990.

"Workers Suggest Solutions." Personnel Journal, February 1991, p. 85.

Zellner, Wendy. "GM's New Teams' Aren't Hitting Any Homers." Business Week, August 8, 1988, pp. 46-47.

Zellner, Wendy. "Chrysler Heads Back to Earth." Business Week, Dec.18, 1989, pp. 46.

Zellner, Wendy. "Top of the News: The Sam's Generation." <u>Business Week</u>, November 25, 1991, pp. 36, 38.

Zemke, Ron, and Schaaf, Dick. <u>The Service Edge: 101 Companies That Profit from Customer Care</u>. New York: Plume, 1990.

"Zenith Moves Jobs to Mexico." <u>Austin American-Statesman,</u> October 30, 1991, p. B6.

Ziegler, Bart. "IBM Declares Independence of Business Units." <u>Austin American-Statesman</u>, November 27, 1991, p. C8-9.

Ziegler, Bart. "Business: GM and IBM: Restructuring Giants." <u>Austin American Statesman</u>, December 18, 1991, p. D1-2.

Zipser, Andy. "Sky's the Limit?" <u>Barron's,</u> September 17, 1990, pp. 16-17.

Zygmont, Jeffrey. "Mapping the Future at Motorola." <u>SKY,</u> November 1992, pp. 61-66.

Index